SHOTS AT SEA

By Tom Lalicki

Shots at Sea: A Houdini & Nate Mystery

Danger in the Dark: A Houdini & Nate Mystery

Grierson's Raid: A Daring Cavalry Strike Through the Heart of the Confederacy

Spellbinder: The Life of Harry Houdini

SHOTS AT SEA

A HOUDINI & NATE MYSTERY

TOM LALICKI

Pictures by **Carlyn Cerniglia**

FARRAR, STRAUS AND GIROUX

NEW YORK

For Jim and Mary Stupple,
always adventurous travelers

Text copyright © 2007 by Tom Lalicki
Pictures copyright © 2007 by Carlyn Cerniglia
All rights reserved
Distributed in Canada by Douglas & McIntyre Ltd.
Printed in the United States of America
Designed by Jay Colvin
First edition, 2007
1 3 5 7 9 10 8 6 4 2

www.fsgkidsbooks.com

Library of Congress Cataloging-in-Publication Data
Lalicki, Tom.
    Shots at sea : a Houdini & Nate mystery / Tom Lalicki ; pictures by
Carlyn Cerniglia.— 1st ed.
        p.   cm.
    Summary: While traveling to England with his mother and great-aunt on
the ocean liner Lusitania in 1911, twelve-year-old Nate, delighted to find
that the Houdinis are also on board, finds himself involved in another
dangerous adventure as he and Houdini try to find the man responsible for
attempting to assassinate another passenger—President Theodore
Roosevelt.
    ISBN-13: 978-0-374-31679-2
    ISBN-10: 0-374-31679-1
    1. Houdini, Harry 1874–1926 —Juvenile fiction.   [1. Houdini, Harry
1874–1926 —Fiction.   2. Roosevelt, Theodore, 1858–1919 —Fiction.
3. Lusitania (Steamship)—Fiction.   4. Magicians—Fiction.   5. Ocean
travel—Fiction.   6. Mystery and detective stories.]   I. Cerniglia, Carlyn,
ill.   II. Title.

PZ7.L1594 Sho 2007
[Fic]—dc22

2006050946

SHOTS AT SEA

Do what you can with what you've got where you are.
—Theodore Roosevelt

Prologue

*A*n idler standing about, day after day, watching other people work. That's Aunt Alice's definition of a loafer, Nate
thought. *A pleasure hound.* The idea troubled Nate but
didn't prevent him from walking south to Fourteenth
Street and west to the Hudson River three mornings in a
row. By the time he reached Pier 54, there were always
dozens of people already gathered.

Many were street vendors, ready to sell the hungry sea-
men sandwiches, fruit, even ice cream. Boys with empty
growlers were poised to fetch beer in the metal pails from
local taverns for a tip. Nate assumed the crowd included a
fair number of pickpockets and confidence men looking

for an easy buck. He kept an eye peeled, hoping to catch one in action.

But most of the crowd just gaped and gawked—for good reason. It took colossal amounts of supplies and human toil to ready the world's largest ship for a crossing from New York to England. Nate had seen the end of the coaling. Twenty-two trains of coal—nearly twelve million pounds—had been unloaded and shoveled belowdecks by hand. To remove the thick, black film of dust left behind, the deck crew hosed and wiped down the entire ship before food could be loaded. Nate counted as one hundred and thirty pigs and one hundred and fifty sheep and lambs were hauled onboard. He stopped counting turkeys, ducks, geese, and pigeons when he overheard a fellow spectator say that the *Lusitania* always stocked over five thousand different fowl in its kitchen.

How many of these people will board with us tomorrow? Nate wondered as he slowly surveyed the crowd. Sizing people up one at a time, he assigned everyone to either the "sailing" or the "not sailing" category. And for each person judged to be sailing, Nate fixed upon a characteristic—a style of dress, a way of standing or walking, a unique facial feature—that would help him identify the person during the voyage.

I'll write to Houdini, if I get enough right.

Nate had met the world's most famous illusionist and his wife by sheer chance—which had proved very lucky for him, his mother, and especially his great-aunt Alice.

She had fallen for the lies of a swindler who intended to take her money and, quite probably, her life, too. But Houdini had teamed up with Nate to expose the criminal's scheme and imprison his gang. In the process, Houdini had taken a shine to the boy because of Nate's powers of observation and his pluck, but they hadn't seen each other for months as the Houdinis toured the country.

Nate made his notes about the people he watched in the red leather-bound journal he had bought to record his thoughts and observations. After all, accurate note-taking skills were essential for any detective. When people didn't fit into either of his original categories, he called them "maybes."

One "maybe" caught his eye because the man was so unusual—eccentric, even. Nate described him as "Tall, young, thin with thinning hair. Walk undistinguished. Circular purple birthmark (wart?) on left nostril." Nate underlined the last sentence, thinking that the man would be easy to recognize with that purple splotch. He looked at "Maybe #3" again.

"Very agitated—always in motion. Wears overcoat (no hat!) even though warm and sunny for October."

How could Nate have known that the man with the purple splotch on his nose and the unnecessary overcoat was concealing a Smith & Wesson New Century revolver? The gun had a four-inch barrel and was loaded with .44-caliber cartridges. A close-range shot to the head or body would invariably kill its target.

Unfamiliar with guns, the man in the overcoat was getting used to the feel of carrying a weapon. He feared that using it was another matter entirely.

The agitated man had test-fired the revolver dozens of times without bullets, but he knew that calmly walking up, leveling the barrel, and firing into the chest of a living human being was . . . terrifying. Terrifying and exciting. *It's my job—my duty,* the man told himself over and over again as he paced around the pier.

Screwing up his courage, the man in the overcoat told himself he *would* board the ship. He *would* track down his prey and execute him. He *would* strike a blow for liberty! For a better, brighter future!

How could Nate have guessed any of it, eager as he was to begin his first great ocean-voyage adventure?

1

Standing at the foot of the gangplank, Nate finally believed they were going. He had made a dozen trips to the tailor, accompanied his mother on numberless shopping excursions for travel necessities, and endured three bon voyage dinners with his aunt's elderly friends. He had even sent a note to Ace Winchell, his onetime partner in crime fighting.

Suitcases, trunks, and hatboxes with enough clothes for his mother and great-aunt Alice—a whole year's worth—were already stowed in the first-class cabin Nate would share with them. At this point, they simply had to climb the narrow, steeply angled wooden gangplank—the first-class gangplank—and follow a ship's steward to their cabin.

But Nate had learned enough about life—the hard way—to value a warning Houdini had given him: "We can never really tell what is ever likely to happen." Nate had climbed only a few steps when he heard his great-aunt's voice below.

"I should not be here, Deborah," she told her niece-in-law, Nate's mother.

"We should go to our cabin. You will feel much better when we settle in," Deborah Fuller replied.

"That is not true. I am far too old for foolishness like this." Aunt Alice shook her head dramatically. "I should never have allowed myself to be bullied and badgered."

"It's just last-minute nerves, Aunt Alice. I have them myself."

"It is not nerves, Deborah, it is clear thinking," Aunt Alice insisted. Nate's mother sighed slightly, searching for the right thing to say.

"Pardon me, ladies," a portly, well-dressed man standing behind them said. "May I be of assistance? If you need help boarding, I will gladly go first and send a steward to aid you."

"I do not need a steward, sir. I need to return to my own home," Aunt Alice said decisively.

"Aunt Alice, let's step aside and let others board while we discuss this," Deborah suggested. "Nate, go ahead and send a steward to us."

"In a flash," Nate said, turning and climbing the gangplank quickly enough to escape his aunt's protests. Touching foot onboard the enormous ship made him quiver with anticipation. He was incredibly eager to explore the length and breadth of every deck of the enormous vessel, but a uniformed officer purposefully blocked his path.

"Your name, sir?" the officer asked in a polite, accented voice. The ship was owned and mostly staffed by Britons.

"Nathaniel Fuller. I am traveling with my mother, Deborah Fuller, and my great-aunt."

The officer flipped through the papers on his clipboard. "And your great-aunt's name is . . . ?"

"Mrs. Ludlow, Mrs. Alice Ludlow."

"Yes, I have the Ludlow-Fuller party in B-6, a three-person saloon-class accommodation on B-deck forward . . ."

"I thought that we were in first class," Nate said. "My aunt can't bear the *thought* of saloons. She certainly isn't going to sleep near one."

"And she will not, my young American gentleman," said the British officer, choking back a laugh. "Our saloon class is the height of luxury, far exceeding your expectation of first class."

"So saloon class doesn't mean saloon, it means first?" Nate asked. "Why not call it first class?"

"Some people think that Americans and British are one people separated by the sharing of a common language," the officer said, as if that answered Nate's question. "But are those two ladies standing by the side of the gangplank your mother and aunt? Why haven't they boarded yet?"

"My aunt is . . . reconsidering the trip."

"A bit late in the day for that, wouldn't you say? Let's go down and sort things out."

"I don't think my going is the best idea. I could never convince my aunt to do anything. Certainly not to change her mind. But I don't think she will let me sail to England by myself."

"I'd take a flyer on that," the officer said, winking for emphasis. Nate was unsure what precisely "taking a flyer" was, but translation could wait.

"You said we are in Cabin B-6?"

"Yes, quite a spacious forward cabin. It's toward the bow on the starboard side—that is the right side, you know—of B-deck," the officer said.

"And *port* is left and the rear is the *stern*," Nate said.

"Jolly good. Now, when I return with your mother and aunt, this steward will guide you."

"No need for that. I can find it myself, after I attend to some business." Nate hotfooted it away, happy to let a stranger lock wills with his great-aunt.

"Business!" an eavesdropping steward whispered skeptically to himself. "The bairn's hardly old enough for long pants. Business indeed!"

2

Having spent his entire life—so far—in the company of Aunt Alice, Nate knew that disappearing from view was the smart thing to do. Every second he lingered near the gangplank, he ran the risk of his aunt digging in her heels. If she had waved her arm and cried, "Nathaniel, come down this instant. We are going home," he couldn't have defied her.

Ducking out was really doing a kindness for his aunt, Nate reasoned. He was just as certain that his mother would not resent his disappearance. She wanted to make this trip as badly as Nate did.

And Aunt Alice *needed* to make the trip. At least that was what her lawyers and friends urged. She had still not completely gotten over the shock of being hoodwinked by a murderer turned medium. *Small wonder!* The charlatan had convinced her that the spirit of Nate's dead father had come back to denounce Nate's mother and demand that Nate be disinherited. Aunt Alice nearly went insane—and she would have been murdered, if Nate and Houdini hadn't saved the day.

Thinking of Houdini reminded Nate that he had a goal in mind: confirming his skills of observation. He had five days before docking in Liverpool, England, to sight all the Pier 54 spectators he had decided were "sailing." Of course, he could never satisfactorily prove the negative. If he failed to see some of the people he had guessed were "not sailing," it did not prove they were not on the ship. It proved that he didn't see them. Sighting the "maybes" would teach him the most.

The word *teach* stung. This was all just an exercise in observation and deduction. Nothing like his life-or-death experiences escaping from a kidnapper and tracking down a murderer before he could strike again. Nate actually missed the fear and panic and sheer excitement he lived through only months ago. It wouldn't ever happen again. Not unless he made hunting criminals his career—a choice he knew his mother would hate.

Even though Nate hadn't seen him since July, he knew that Houdini understood. Why else would Houdini have loaned Nate his own heavily annotated copies of *Professional Criminals of America* and *Recollections of a New York*

City Chief of Police—two great basic textbooks about crime and deduction? And all the Sherlock Holmes novels Nate bought at the used book stalls on Fourth Avenue were instructive.

But Nate's favorite was Houdini's own book *The Right Way to Do Wrong: An Exposé of Successful Criminals.* Nate had read it at least five times, learning scads about burglars, pickpockets, jewel thieves, and swindlers of all sorts.

Deep in thought, reviewing the entries in his journal, Nate was oblivious to the hurly-burly surrounding him in the grand hallway of the *Lusitania*'s main deck.

"Beggin' your pardon, sir," a strongly accented voice broke in, "this isn't the *best* place to have a quiet read."

Nate looked up, around, and finally down before locating the speaker. He was a boy probably no older than Nate himself—twelve, *maybe* even thirteen—but quite a bit shorter. In his tight-fitting blue uniform with two collar-to-waist rows of shiny buttons, the boy clearly was a crew member.

"I could guide you to your cabin or point you to the proper reading lounge, if you like," the boy offered.

"Are you a steward? Your uniform isn't like the others," Nate remarked.

"I hope, one day, sir, to be a steward. But that's years away. I am a bellboy at present."

"You carry people's bags to their rooms? That's what bellboys do at hotels," Nate said.

"We do what is called for. 'Men of all work,' you might say. Keep the ship running, really. We deliver wireless messages from the radio room, carry messages between passengers, hunt up extra blankets for people sitting in the deck chairs. We even walk dogs—that's the best tipping," he added confidentially.

Nate wanted to hear more. He wanted to tell the bellboy about his job last summer as a dogsbody for Bennett & Son, Gentlemen's Hatters, of Fifth Avenue. But he didn't do either. He'd been told—time and again—not to be familiar with the crew.

"English servants are different," Aunt Alice had repeatedly said to him. "They know their place, and they expect you to know your place. Be dignified and authoritative, Nephew."

"Is B-6 this way?" Nate asked lamely, already knowing the answer.

"Facing the bow, sir. Starboard."

"Thanks. That's all I need to know."

"I can show you the way," the bellboy said while gesturing toward the gigantic double stairway in the center of the room. "We could take the lift."

"Lift?"

"The electric lift, there in between the stairs," the bellboy said, pointing to an open-air cage made entirely of wrought iron.

"Oh, the elevator," Nate said. At just that moment the

full passenger compartment came into view and glided silently down to floor level. "So you call it a lift?"

"That's what it does, sir, lifts people," the bellboy said matter-of-factly.

"It does, but not me. I'll take the stairs," Nate said happily.

"Suit yourself, sir."

3

It pleased Nate to be on his own, exploring the ship. By the time he passed the crowded windows of the Enquiry Desk and climbed one of the wide stairways up to D-deck, he realized that there were just too many passengers sightseeing for his purposes.

To Nate's right—toward the ship's bow—the narrow passageway was frantic with activity. As passengers moved themselves and their baggage into cabins, earlier arrivals were milling about, peeking into open cabin doors and making introductions to their neighbors. To Nate's left was the entrance to the first-class dining room. A look around the vast room revealed dozens of circular and rectangular tables, each with six to twelve matching chairs. Looking upward, Nate realized that the room had a second dining level on the deck above. High above, three decks up, was an enormous white dome covered with gold woodworking and oval paintings.

With no particular aim in mind—other than *not* finding his cabin until after the ship was safely out of New York harbor—Nate wandered from deck to deck. He passed a generously sized library with dozens of writing desks. There were both men's barbershops and ladies' hair salons already doing a brisk business. He passed a typewriter room, in which several men were dictating to female typists, and a radio room, where passengers could compose messages to be sent wirelessly at great expense—seven dollars for ten words, said the sign. It also gave the price in British pounds and shillings, and in other foreign money symbols that Nate didn't know.

Having reached the top deck, A-deck, Nate strolled onto the grand first-class promenade, a walkway at least fifteen feet wide that seemed to run the entire perimeter of the ship, a great elongated oval shape. On the inside were the exterior walls of passenger cabins and other public rooms. On the outside—the edge of the deck near the water—there was a four-foot-high metal railing.

Nate couldn't get a clear view of the water everywhere because huge lifeboats hung from metal arms near the bow and stern. He counted the lifeboats and tried to imagine thousands of people in them. Even though math was his worst subject in school, Nate was pretty sure that everyone onboard couldn't fit in these.

Nate was on the side of the promenade facing Pier 54. He looked down, scanning the gangplank area for his mother and great-aunt. Unable to find them, he happily concluded they were both onboard.

Bonggg! Bonggg!

"Final call to go ashore," announced a steward strolling by. He struck the small gong he carried twice more with a padded mallet and continued spreading his message. "All visitors and guests begin to disembark now. The *Lusitania* will depart in fifteen minutes."

Previous announcements had caused little stir, but upon hearing this final call, visitors flooded toward the gangplanks, saying their final goodbyes to passengers with kisses, embraces, and handshakes. On the pier, thousands of well-wishers were waving upward. Passengers were jostling Nate for space at the railing, eager to wave back to family, friends, and total strangers.

Since Nate had nobody to wave to—his entire family was onboard—he squirmed through the pressing throng and walked sternward, toward the less crowded section of the promenade.

He was surprised to discover that the promenade deck did not actually loop the ship uninterrupted. The last portion of the walkway, at the stern, was intentionally separated from the much larger part he was standing on. It was as if someone had sawed the deck into two unequal pieces and pulled them away from each other.

As he leaned against the rail, Nate guessed that the distance to the rail of the smaller stern section was six or seven feet. Looking over the rail, he saw that the deck really was interrupted. Separating the two promenades was a drop of at least twenty feet. He realized that if you fell over the railing on A-deck, you would land on C-deck.

The smaller section of the promenade deck was intensely crowded. Passengers were standing five and six deep, craning to wave at friends on the pier. Wondering about this curious division, Nate thought he heard a familiar voice calling him.

4

"Will wonders *never* cease?"

Nate recognized the woman's voice, high-pitched and giddy, cutting through the clamor. It had to be Mrs. Houdini. He scanned the much smaller promenade area.

"So, Mr. Nathaniel Greene Makeworthy Fuller the Fourth, you do not recognize your old friend Bess Houdini?"

Looking away from the crowd, he saw her: a tiny, slim woman about the same age as his mother. A wide-brimmed hat festooned with artificial flowers shielded her face from the sun but did not hide her affectionate smile.

"Mrs. Houdini, what are you doing here? Is Houdini here, too? Why are you over there? How can I get across?"

"So many questions! Stay right there. I will send Phineas to fetch you."

"Phineas?" Nate asked. That was a name he had never heard.

"No more questions now," she yelled as the earsplitting horns of the *Lusitania* announced that the ship was finally leaving New York Harbor. Mrs. Houdini made a series of hand gestures—a regular pantomime—indicating that Nate should stay put, and then she vanished into the crowd.

Wondering who Phineas was, Nate recalled that it took Mrs. Houdini no time at all to turn strangers into friends. Last summer, Nate had first gone to the Houdinis' Upper West Side brownstone to collect an unpaid Bennett & Son bill and moments later found himself telling Mrs. Houdini his family history.

Nate couldn't stay put as the great ocean liner slowly slid out from the pier. It was exactly three o'clock, Tuesday, October 10, 1911, when the ship eased out of its berth. Dense, grayish black smoke billowed from only one of the ship's four tall smokestacks at first. Then smoke shot up through two more, and the ship began to make a hard left turn. The *Lusitania* eased to the left until it had made a full one hundred and eighty degrees. The bow now faced down the Hudson River, toward the ocean. The crowd on deck thinned considerably. Nate surmised that those who had left were experienced sailors, no longer interested in watching a ship maneuver into open water.

"Mr. Fuller, are you?" asked a boy while he touched Nate's arm lightly. It was another bellboy, this one about Nate's height and age, he thought. His innocent, watery green eyes and densely freckled face were offset by a posture and expression Nate recognized—street tough, possibly street mean, too.

"Are you Phineas?"

"Ow!" he said with a wince. "That's the name me mum gave me. Mrs. 'Oodini dragged it outa me."

"What should I call you?"

"Newborn."

"Well . . . I'm not sure I want to call you by your last name, either. And I don't want to call you Bellboy."

"It's a situation you'll 'ave to noodle on, ain't it, sir? Now, follow me an' I'll lead you to Mrs. 'Oodini."

"Lead on," Nate said enthusiastically. "Where are we going, by the way?"

"To the second-class stairway," Newborn said as Nate followed him toward the center of the ship.

"But we're walking *away* from Mrs. Houdini."

"Unless you want to jump the gap, that's what you 'ave to do," Newborn replied scornfully.

"I don't understand," Nate said.

"You are a saloon-class passenger, sir, and the 'Oodinis

is second-class." As they descended the grand stairway, Nate waited to hear more, but Newborn's statement seemed to have settled the matter to the bellboy's satisfaction.

"Do you mean I'm not supposed to socialize with Mrs. Houdini because we're not traveling in the same *class*?"

"Exactly."

"But *why*?"

"Look 'ere, sir," Newborn said as he stopped and turned to face Nate. "If you buy a first-class train ticket, you don't sit in a second-class carriage, now do you?"

"We don't have first- or second-class tickets on the subway or the El in New York. You sit wherever you like."

"Very irregular," the bellboy muttered. They continued in silence as they walked back toward the stern and finally reached the second-class stairway.

"Everything's quite irregular with these 'Oodinis," Newborn said as they climbed the plainer, narrower second-class stairway.

"Because they are exceptional. Unique," Nate said. *They are unique. And they are my friends,* he thought proudly.

"But the classes aren't supposed to mix now, are they, sir?"

"Why not?" Nate asked. He wondered if the bellboy shared his aunt Alice's point of view.

"Why not, sir? Because the first-class passengers aren't supposed to be bothered by second-class passengers like the 'Oodinis. And they sure don't want to mix with the steerage lot—those we call 'third-class' passengers now, to make them seem more grand."

"But *I* want to mix with the Houdinis."

"Of course you do, sir. Don't everybody on this ship? 'Oodini is famous as the King of England and rich as an earl, ain't 'e? Makes it *very* irregular that 'e and 'is missus travel second-class. Second's for the likes of dodgy solicitors an' out-to-pasture chokers, not flash music hall types like 'Oodini—"

Nate tried to interrupt, but the bellboy was on a verbal tear.

"—What kerfuffle! Go wherever they like, they can—that's straight from the captain. I bet 'Oodini'll even eat with the captain. 'Ow's someone like me to keep it all straight, I ask you?"

Nate thought about it, but their circuitous journey—down three decks, across the ship, and back up two—ended before he had anything worth saying.

" 'Ere's the second-class ladies' drawing room; Mrs. 'Oodini's waitin'."

5

There she was, in a wing chair at a table for two. The bright, multiwindowed room was nearly filled with women sharing tea and listening to a steward play an upright piano. Mrs. Houdini eagerly beckoned Nate to take a seat.

"It is *such* a joy to see you, Nate. We must all get together—your mother, your aunt, if she is willing—"

"But how did you recognize me, Mrs. Houdini? Sorry to interrupt, but how?"

"Am I not as magical and mysterious as my husband?" she asked, her eyes twinkling. Nate had seen that look often enough last summer to know she was pulling his leg.

"Every bit as magical and mysterious," he replied with mock solemnity. "And it's criminal of me to ask."

Mrs. Houdini paused; the playfulness in her expression was tempered by a flush of warmth, of affection. "How quickly you've aged."

"I'm *still* not thirteen yet," Nate said.

"Not in years, no. But you are a different young man from the one who sat in my kitchen last summer."

"I suppose that's natural, Mrs. Houdini . . . given all that happened."

They noticed a waiter standing patiently above them. Mrs. Houdini told Nate she would love tea. It took Nate a few seconds to remember that he should order for the lady, but he recovered admirably, ordering tea for one and orange juice for himself.

"I do owe you an explanation," Mrs. Houdini continued. "It has been such a busy year, hardly ever at home." She began to catalog their travels, but Nate needed no recapping. He and his mother had followed Houdini's exploits through the newspapers—no longer banned from the house by Aunt Alice.

In Detroit, Houdini had escaped from a larger-than-life envelope. It was twelve feet high and five feet wide, woven from heavy rope fiber and held together by hundreds of steel rivets. Houdini, within the privacy of his "Ghost Cabinet," a triangular screen of black fabric panels, struggled for less than twenty minutes before freeing himself. The giant envelope was, of course, completely undamaged.

In Kansas City, a group of mail carriers stuffed Houdini into a standard-size canvas mailbag. The bag was cinched together with a heavy leather strap and secured by a combination lock. The theater's orchestra repeated "My Country, 'Tis of Thee" for twenty-one minutes until Houdini emerged from his Ghost Cabinet with the bag, strap, and combination lock in hand—none of them damaged.

The papers reported a number of benefit performances Houdini gave at various children's hospitals, orphanages, and prisons. But the most remarkable was a Chicago performance to benefit the family of a pioneer aviator whose plane had crashed. Houdini, handcuffed and leg-shackled, was thrown into Lake Michigan from an airplane. More than ten thousand spectators waited for six heart-pounding minutes before the escape artist popped to the surface, free and unharmed.

"Oh, did you enjoy those crime books Houdini sent you?" Mrs. Houdini asked, interrupting herself.

"Very much. I returned them all, too. And sent Houdini a letter thanking him for thinking of me."

"*Ach*, your letter is undoubtedly in the box of correspondence we brought onboard. We had a hectic time making this boat. We had planned to cross next week on *Die Kronprinzessin Cecilie*."

Bess Houdini seemed to notice Nate's brow furrowing, a cue that she had lapsed into the native German her family spoke when she was a child.

"The *Crown Princess Cecile* in English. It is a lavish new German liner. *Wahrhaftig*, Houdini has no fondness for the German kaiser or his crown princess, but Cecilia is Houdini's *mother's* name. Houdini is ever so sentimental about his mother."

"Why did you switch to the *Lusitania?*"

"To see *you*, Nate. *And* your darling mother."

"Really! To see us!" Nate felt his astonishment quickly overwhelmed by satisfaction.

"Really! Your mother and I have exchanged letters. When she told me you were definitely traveling on this ship, Houdini insisted we change our plans. He also insisted that your mother keep it as a surprise, just in case."

"Because we can never really tell what is likely to happen."

"Nate, I warn you," Mrs. Houdini began sternly, "do not quote my husband to himself. His head is quite swelled enough."

As they enjoyed the joke, the waiter served their drinks. Mrs. Houdini poured her tea through a strainer, catching the loose tea leaves. Nate was grateful she hadn't asked him to pour.

"Is the bellboy who brought me here working for you?" Nate asked.

"Phineas? Yes. We need a person to walk Charlie and run errands."

"I could do that," Nate broke in. "I love your dog."

"That is not done, Nate. Etiquette requires that you follow the rules."

"I hope I can get the hang of it. For example, I can't see why it's 'irregular' for us to visit."

"Someone said that to you?"

"Phineas."

"Ah . . . he is a bit rough around the edges," Bess said thoughtfully. "Not as well-spoken—or polite—as crew members normally are."

"Why did you hire him to walk Charlie?"

"That is Houdini's doing. I think Phineas reminds Houdini of himself at that age."

Nate considered that, trying to imagine Houdini as a boy. He also wondered why the Houdinis traveled in second class. But asking would be too rude, and he liked Bess Houdini far too much to risk being rude.

"After dinner tonight, why don't you do some sleuthing? 'Get the goods' on Phineas. Is that the way to say it?"

"That's one way to say it," Nate replied. "But how will I get the goods on him?"

"That is part of your second surprise today. As we boarded, Houdini received a message inviting him to a 'men-only' after-dinner constitutional."

"Constitutional? A walk around the deck?"

"That is it, and Houdini wants you to trail behind the men with Phineas and Charlie. It will give you the perfect opportunity to question Phineas about his background."

"But couldn't I walk *with* Houdini and the others? I can talk to Phineas anytime."

"Unfortunately, Houdini cannot simply invite you along. The man who invited him is too important, too famous, to take liberties with."

"More famous than Houdini?" Nate asked, genuinely puzzled.

"More famous even than Houdini—such a person really does exist."

6

Nate was curious to learn who the mystery passenger was, but he couldn't coax any clues from Mrs. Houdini. She did tell Nate where Houdini was—in their cabin— and why. He was afraid of seasickness.

Houdini could jump from tall bridges—even from airplanes—into freezing water with no problem at all. But the rocking of a ship on the ocean incapacitated him. Bess told Nate that her husband often stayed in their cabin for an entire crossing, eating nothing but ice chips and lemonade. He became delirious on one trip, so disoriented that his wife feared for his safety. She tied him to the bunk with rope, but knowing he could undo the knots, she strapped a life preserver to his chest—just in case he fell overboard.

Houdini hoped that the world's largest ship, a ship half again larger than the biggest battleship, would provide a smooth journey. Until he was sure, however, the world-famed entertainer sorted unopened mail and unpacked books and clothes in his cabin.

It was nearly five when Bess Houdini and Nate parted. Fearing the worst, Nate slowly made his way back to B-deck and located the interior corridor, or "alleyway" in shipboard language, that led to his stateroom. He tapped on the door of Cabin B-6 and slowly opened it. His fears proved groundless. If his disappearance had irritated Aunt Alice, it was now forgotten.

His mother never mentioned it. She insisted on giving him a guided tour of their stateroom even though there was barely space for two people to stand side by side. She pointed out the ample clothes storage, the double-decker bed against one wall that she and Aunt Alice would occupy, and the settee opposite, where Nate would sleep. There were ceiling-to-floor privacy curtains for each, and a tiny washroom at the back of the cabin.

Aunt Alice, never once asking why Nate had disappeared, admitted that she regretted not getting a more luxurious stateroom—one with full bathroom facilities.

As Nate struggled into the unfamiliar evening clothes he was required to wear at dinner, he decided that his great-aunt might actually be enjoying herself.

His mother seemed to read his thoughts. "This trip is going to be a tonic for all of us, especially Aunt Alice," she said, helping Nate knot his black bow tie. "And you, my son, you look as grand as Houdini. I hope you liked your surprise." Smiling, she added, "You look as handsome in evening dress as your father."

Dinner itself was unbelievably grand. The meal offered too many courses—appetizers, soup, a fish course, a meat course, dessert, fruit and cheese—and far too many choices for each course. And there was too much to see to concentrate on food.

Sitting on the second tier of the dining saloon, they had a perfect view of the floor below. A band played, and waiters glided at breakneck speed with huge trays. Every woman Nate fixed on seemed more colorfully dressed than the one before. They wore shining satins and silks in a rainbow of colors. They had elaborate hairdos, wore bright red lip and cheek makeup. Some almost sagged under the weight of necklaces, tiaras, and other jewelry. Alongside each woman sat a man in a regulation penguin suit just like Nate's.

The boy realized that his family was out of place. Aunt Alice wore a high-collared, pleated dress that might have been a hundred years old, or close to it. Nate's mother wore no jewelry or makeup. He knew that her dress was not stylish, either, but he thought she looked elegant nonetheless.

During the fish course, all heads turned as the captain

33

welcomed special guests to his table. The room buzzed when Houdini and his wife were seated. The buzz grew even louder when Mrs. Houdini's mystery guest seated himself. He *was* even more famous than Houdini: he was Teddy Roosevelt.

As if answering a question on a history test, Nate ticked off the great man's accomplishments: former president of the United States, builder of the Panama Canal, creator of the national park system, champion of pure food and medicine, enemy of child labor, Nobel Peace Prize winner. But one accomplishment stuck in Nate's throat.

Teddy Roosevelt: liberator of Cuba, the man who had inspired Nate's father to leave his wife, abandon his law practice, become a soldier, and die from typhoid fever long before the Rough Riders' glorious charge up San Juan Hill.

7

Looking at the eight men ahead as they started another loop of the grand promenade, Nate observed that Houdini certainly stood out from the crowd. Even a crowd that included former President Roosevelt.

Houdini was the shortest man in the group and the most distinctive. His huge, hatless head was crowned by wild, wiry hair. Still dressed in a black frock coat with high-collared shirt, he was quite formal. The others had changed from evening attire into comfortable tweeds and snap-brim hats suitable for exercise. Nate—at less than thirteen—was still considered a child. Far too young for more than one suit, in Aunt Alice's opinion. He had changed into the twenty-dollar blue serge Brooks Brothers suit that had been purchased for his all-around, day in and day out, wear.

Nate thought that Houdini looked ready to jump on-stage and thunder out his call to attention: "Layyyy-deees and Gen-tell-men!" *Maybe this stroll with President Roosevelt really is a performance of some sort.*

Nate couldn't follow the conversation he overheard. It was mostly about European politics and the possibilities of war. And he needed to get the goods on Phineas for Mrs. Houdini, anyway.

"So, Phineas," he began quietly.

"It's Newborn, sir. Or plain Phin if you aim to be a mate." The bellboy's arm was suddenly yanked straight out, fighting against a surprisingly powerful force pulling him forward. Charlie, the Houdinis' terrier, struggled to catch up with his master.

"Poor Charlie, you can't understand why you're not a member of the party," Nate consoled. The white-and-brown terrier tossed his head back and yipped, as if to acknowledge his frustration.

"So you know the dog, too, eh?" Phin asked. "Are you related to the 'Oodinis?"

"Just friends," Nate said.

"Neighbors is it, somethin' like that?"

Not answering, Nate tried to get *his* investigation back on track.

"How did the Houdinis pick you to watch Charlie? There must be a hundred other bellboys on this ship."

"That's me uncle's doin'. A senior steward 'e is," said Phin proudly.

"He picked you to work for the Houdinis?"

"Spot on! 'E sees they're wantin' a dog walker an' says, 'I been a steward near on fifteen years, eh, and I knows there's some who tips and some who don't. And it don't take no bleedin' foxhound to see the 'Oodinis is tippers.' "

Before Nate could think of a response, a change in the direction of the other conversation pricked up his ears.

"Houdini, you *are* an expert on the otherworldly—*Spiritualism* and all that," Roosevelt said, flashing a smile so broad that his teeth shone like a beacon in the dim light. "I *must* have your opinion on the subject of mental telepathy."

"I'd be dee-lighted, Mr. President!" Houdini chuffed, using an expression Roosevelt had made famous around the world. "Are you a believer yourself?"

"What a perfect corker you are, Houdini, answering my question with your own. Afraid to come clean?"

"On the contrary, Mr. President. I am afraid to bore you with too much information about a subject I have studied so long."

"Perfectly sensible," Roosevelt replied. "Can psychics really read people's thoughts? I think there is much in it that we presently do not understand. The only trouble is that it usually gets mixed up with all kinds of fakes."

"What an extraordinary insight, Mr. President. There *may* be much we do not understand. I have never actually witnessed real telepathy—thoughts transferred from one mind to another. I have seen it faked quite well. Mrs. Houdini and I once earned our living that way, to our shame."

Nate was taken aback by the notion that the Houdinis would do anything shameful, but Houdini's admission vanished into the night like cigar smoke in the face of the stiff wind blowing across the deck.

"So you deny mental telepathy?" Roosevelt asked.

"Mr. President, you've seen gazelles, zebras, and all manner of exotic animals that I have never witnessed. I would not deny they exist because I have not seen them. On the other hand, since neither I nor anyone I trust has *ever* seen a unicorn, it would be foolish of me to say scientifically that unicorns exist."

"Bully for you, Mr. Houdini!" Roosevelt said gleefully. "Are all séances phony?"

"I try to keep an open mind."

"You admit that there is a *possibility* of communicating with people who have died?"

"There is."

"Capital!" Roosevelt exclaimed. "Will you give us a little séance one night?"

"I am not a medium, Mr. President. I have no supernatural powers," Houdini said most earnestly.

"Let *us* be the judges!" The former president looked round to his walking companions for support. All agreed loudly that a séance was just what the doctor ordered to liven up the trip.

"Forgive me," Houdini said, "but *I will not* hold a séance. I will most gladly give a *psychical* demonstration—during the fancy-dress party—the night before we dock in Liverpool. Is that acceptable, Mr. President?"

Roosevelt looked skeptical. "You don't mean card tricks or the like, do you? Several of your colleagues performed sleight of hand at the White House . . . They quite amused the children."

"But you were not mystified."

"Drat, I was not."

"Mr. President, you challenge me to devise an exceptional demonstration, so . . . let it be known . . ."

Houdini's voice rose before he paused dramatically. He seemed to savor the near-silence on the moonlit ship's deck.

"—I accept your Presidential Challenge and will work night and day to create an illusion that will leave you *speechless*, even *breathless!*"

Roosevelt laughed and shook Houdini's hand as several men patted Houdini's back in approval.

"A brassy character this 'Oodini is," Phin said to Nate.

"If by 'brassy' you mean confident, he is. And has every right to be. Just wait until you see what Houdini does."

"You've seen this trick, then?"

"No . . . I have no idea what the demonstration will be. It will be brilliant, that's all I—"

"Ow!" the dog walker interrupted. "The little brute's

39

been doin' 'is business," Phin said, nodding toward a fresh pile of dog waste on the wooden deck.

Charlie tugged at his leash and yelped impatiently. Houdini and his party were nearly out of sight.

"I'll take Charlie for a while," offered Nate.

"But see 'ere, I'll catch it if I let go of the dog," Phin protested.

"You won't. Charlie and I are old friends," Nate said, grabbing the terrier's leash.

"Gor, don't let him run wild," Phin pleaded as he knelt down to clean up the mess.

Phin's prompt action helped Nate recognize just how different living on a ship was from living in a city. The air was always brisk and tangy, but not just because the *Lusitania* was steaming forward, its bow rising and dipping through the ocean. The air was fresh thanks to the lack of sweating horses and piles of manure and jostling people who rarely bathed or changed their clothes.

When Charlie tugged anxiously at his lead, Nate saw that the walking party was nearly out of sight. Giving the terrier his lead, they quickly regained a position at the rear of the walking party. Nate observed that one member of the main group was lagging, as if pacing himself to stay behind the rest.

Is that fellow falling behind because he cannot keep up the pace?

Seeing that the trailing man stayed a constant distance behind the main group, Nate discarded that idea.

"Observe, evaluate, observe again, and reevaluate" was advice Houdini had given Nate more than once.

Nate concentrated. He counted the men walking ahead.

There are nine of them; I'm sure there were only eight before. This "new man" must have slipped in behind them while Newborn and I were talking. But why?

Nate observed the new man more closely. He wore a hat with the brim pulled down and an overcoat with the collar up, although the night air was warm.

The man was tall, thin, with a bushy beard and a long, pointed nose. He certainly hadn't been with the Roosevelt group earlier, but something about him was familiar. Nate couldn't tell exactly what, though.

Was he trying to hide his face? Why did he keep one hand, not both, in his pocket?

"All right, I'll take the dog's lead," said Phin, done cleaning up after Charlie.

"Mr. Roosevelt!" the man in the overcoat called loudly. He drew his hand out of his pocket, and Nate saw the glint of shiny metal. The man dropped his arm straight down and held it close to his body.

It's a gun! He has a gun!

"Mr. Roosevelt, a word with you, please."

The former president stopped and turned, leaning forward and squinting.

The man in the overcoat raised his right arm and cupped his left hand underneath the right.

"He's got a gun! He's got a gun!" Nate shouted, and rushed toward the assailant.

A flash of pale fire and smoke and the explosive crack of a shot froze the moment. Nate stared in disbelief.

He's shot the president!

8

The momentary stillness was broken by a groan of pain. Nate looked past the gunman and saw a man's body being lowered to the deck by the walking party. Shouts of "Murder!" and "Get a doctor!" and "Stop that man!" filled the air. The assassin had not moved an inch. His arms were locked in shooting position.

Houdini pushed aside several of his companions and walked deliberately toward the gunman. He was no more than three paces away when another shot cracked.

The impact spun Houdini nearly in a circle. He dropped to one knee, clutching the side of his chest, and looked up at the shooter. The gunman's arm was still outstretched, smoke wafting around the brim of his hat.

Houdini struggled to his feet but could not move forward. He lurched to his right and staggered into a deck chair before falling to the ground. The sight of his master injured was more than Charlie could stand. The dog broke into a run so violent that he yanked the leash from Phin's hand and dashed to Houdini's side.

"Drop your gun, sir," the fallen Houdini panted, trying to make eye contact with the assassin. "You've done what you came to do. Don't hurt any more people."

Houdini's words moved the gunman. He brought the revolver down to his side, pocketed it, and turned to walk away.

That brought him face-to-face with Nate and the bell-boy. Houdini, no doubt sensing catastrophe, shouted: "Nate, stand aside! Let him pass!"

Suddenly alert, the shooter looked toward Nate and Phin. He walked double time, veering away from the boys and toward the door that led to the grand stairway.

Nate was on the move quickly, running diagonally to intercept the shooter. Reaching the doorway first, he raised his hands and heard himself say: "Surrender! You can't escape."

Bravery proved no match for fear and cunning. The shooter struck without warning. He threw a vicious punch into Nate's stomach with his free hand. Nate crumpled backward against the door, gasping for air.

Frantically struggling to stay upright, he grasped the frame of the door.

The gunman paused and stared, as if in admiration of the boy's tenacity. But the sound of onrushing feet and angry voices from all directions seemed to spur him into action. Pulling the revolver from his coat again, he held the barrel in the palm of his hand. Raising it, he swung back and then raked the handle across the back of Nate's head. His blow dropped Nate to the deck. Powerless, the boy watched the gunman step over him and escape through the door.

The promenade deck quickly filled with people. Passengers flooded from the lounge, from the smoking room, from cabins near the shootings. Crew members tried to keep order. A man with a medical bag, followed by a uniformed nurse, nearly tripped over Nate before realizing he was injured.

"I'm the ship's doctor. Have you been shot?" he asked, kneeling over Nate.

"No," Nate answered, unable to say more.

"That's a nasty gash you have," the doctor said while examining Nate's scalp. "You will be fine," he advised, digging a bandage from his bag, "but I thought someone had been shot."

"Over here!" said Phin, pointing toward the main party.

"Nurse, pressure-bandage his head and then follow me," the doctor ordered as he rushed toward Roosevelt and Houdini.

Questions flooded into Nate's mind: *Is Houdini dead? Is President Roosevelt dead? Why didn't I see that punch coming? What will Aunt Alice say?*

"A royal cock-up this is, eh?"

Nate looked up to see Phin shaking his head.

"Leave it to you Yanks to turn a walk in the park into the blinkin' shoot-out at the O.K. Corral."

9

Help did not arrive for Nate all that soon. The *Lusitania* had a fully equipped hospital, complete with separate wards for ladies and gentlemen. But the ship's excellent medical staff usually treated seasickness and gastritis, not gunshot victims. Propped up near the doorway, Nate woozily watched a crowd of curious passengers gathered around the other victims while Phin kept him company.

"Make way! Make way!" called a voice of authority. The doctor walked ahead of a stretcher carried by two stewards.

Nate assumed it carried President Roosevelt.

Next came the nurse, her pointed cap nearly sideways on her head. Behind her was another stretcher.

"I can walk, I assure you," the patient insisted.

"Houdini?" Nate cried out as the stretcher came near. Charlie walked behind it, whining pitifully.

"Nate, is that you?" The voice was weak but clearly Houdini's. Phin was quick-witted enough to dash behind the medical party, grab Charlie's leash, and pull him back toward Nate.

"Are you badly wounded?" the escapologist's young friend asked.

"It's nothing, a trifle." As the stretcher passed, Houdini said, "He hurt my hanky-panky stuff worse than he did me."

"Hurt my hanky-panky stuff?" a bewildered Nate repeated to himself.

"By thunder, this boy is hurt!"

Nate turned to see who the speaker with the high-pitched, excited voice was. He was a powerful-looking man with a full gray mustache and pince-nez spectacles perched on his nose. His face was scrunched as he squinted to get a better look at Nate.

"President Roosevelt?" asked Nate in disbelief. "But you were shot. I saw it."

"Not I, alas. A brave man took the bullet for me. I pray that he recovers."

Nate tried to remember the lightning-fast chain of

events and realized that he had not seen the shooting. His eyes had never left the gunman.

"I say, are *you* the one who called out the warning?" Roosevelt asked. "Are you Houdini's *protégé*?"

"I guess I am, if that's what Houdini calls me."

"Capital! A very bright boy you are. You saved my life."

"But what about the man who was shot? Who is he? Will he live?"

"You are *exceedingly* curious for a wounded man," Roosevelt said brightly. "Let's get you some medical attention. Bellboy, is that the Houdinis' dog?" he asked Phin.

"It is, Your Excellency," Phin replied grandly.

"Pish! I am not . . . Do you know where Houdini's stateroom is?"

"I do, Your Excel— sir. I walk the dog for 'em."

"Then go there at once, by George, and tell Mrs. Houdini that her husband was wounded. Be careful not to alarm her unduly—the wound is *not* life-threatening. Do you understand?" Roosevelt said, staring intently.

"Right as rain, sir." Phin had turned about-face, eager to leave, when Roosevelt called him back.

"Enlist another bellboy or steward to inform this young man's father that he is in the hospital—very slightly injured," he ordered.

"I'm not traveling with my father, Mr. President. I am with my mother and aunt," Nate said.

"But I don't know your cabin number," Phin explained.

"It's B-6." As an afterthought, Nate said, "Be sure to tell my mother it's nothing. A trifle."

"Admirably considerate," Roosevelt remarked, bending to help Nate to his feet. A ship's officer who had been standing passively nearby joined in. Supporting Nate on both sides, they walked toward the hospital.

10

It was not far to the ship's hospital—down two decks and one hundred feet astern, past the Officers' Mess, where the chief crew members dined—but it was a long trip nonetheless. News of the shootings on A-deck had raced like wildfire in a tinder-dry forest. The curious had abandoned their bridge and billiard games, left behind their after-dinner brandy and cigars, and were prowling the decks for information. Each time they were stopped by a party of two or three passengers, Roosevelt reassured them that he was unharmed, thanked them for their concern, and stressed that Nate—the boy with the bandaged head—needed medical attention.

No sooner had they trudged forward a few paces than

another group confronted them and the scene was re-played. Roosevelt showed unflagging good humor, repeating the same words again and again, but making it sound fresh and sincere each time.

When they finally ducked into the quiet alleyway leading to the hospital, the former president uttered an appeal to no one in particular: "I pray that Flanagan survives."

"Is that the man who was shot, Mr. President?" asked Nate. "You know him?"

"Very well," Roosevelt replied. "Tommy Flanagan was a member of the White House Police Department—one of the men assigned to protect the president and his family. He came to the White House days after I did. We both retired at nearly the same time."

"Mr. Flanagan is your bodyguard?" Nate asked.

"I need no *bodyguards*, young man." Roosevelt flared, his face flushing deep red. "When I am traveling without my family, it is agreeable to have a friend along with me. But I am exceedingly able to care for myself! Let's get your wound attended to."

Nate wondered whether the gunman had shot Flanagan accidentally or whether the *ex*-bodyguard had heard Nate's warning and stepped in front of the bullet's intended victim.

Walking through the doorway of the ship's hospital, Nate was surprised to see Houdini sitting up in bed and to

hear a squabble in progress between the injured entertainer, his wife, and the captain.

"The fact is, sir, if I did not have it on good authority
that you are an honest man, I would have you confined to
your cabin for the rest of the voyage," puffed Captain
Railsback, a heavyset man with wavy salt-and-pepper hair
and matching full beard. The creases on his immaculate
trousers were sharp enough to cut a breakfast roll.

"Captain, my husband has just had a bullet removed from his side. Be kind enough not to irritate
him—or me—with such utter nonsense," Mrs. Houdini
said icily.

"Houdini! What bull luck you have!" Roosevelt called
out enthusiastically, interrupting the row.

All eyes turned toward the door. Deborah Fuller,
seated in a chair on the opposite side of the room, saw her
son and rushed forward.

"Nate, I've been so worried. Are you all right?"

"I'm fine," Nate said.

"That bandage . . . Doctor, please look at my son!"

Roosevelt relinquished one of Nate's arms to a nurse.
She and the silent ship's officer walked Nate into an examining room off the main ward, followed by his mother.
There the nurse irrigated his wound and determined that
it was superficial. Once Nate showed that he could count
the doctor's fingers and keep his eyes on the doctor's
moving hand, Mrs. Fuller was informed that her son

would be perfectly fit after the swelling went down and the gash healed.

"So Houdini will recover, too?" Nate asked the doctor.

"Indeed he will." The doctor laughed. "He's what you might call a man who makes his own luck."

"What about Mr. Flanagan?"

"He is seriously wounded. But we are fortunate to have one of the finest London surgeons traveling with us. He is operating in the surgery down the hall as we speak."

With that, the doctor escorted the boy and his mother into the main ward. After the doctor exchanged introductions with President Roosevelt and updated him on Flanagan's condition, the captain resumed his harangue against Houdini.

"The way you outfit yourself is *very* suspicious, Mr. Houdini. I could have you banned from every ship plying the Atlantic, sir, if I chose to do so."

"Would you prefer that my husband was shot dead?" Mrs. Houdini asked angrily.

"Good lord, man! What has Houdini done to excite you so?" Roosevelt asked.

"When my husband rushed forward to capture the assassin who shot at you, Mr. Roosevelt, the bullet that struck him mercifully passed through a deck of cards Houdini had inside his coat pocket," Mrs. Houdini said.

"Hidden decks of cards! Shameful!" said Captain Railsback.

Mrs. Houdini glared at him for several tense seconds

before continuing. "The bullet's force was so spent that it penetrated only a short way into Houdini's flesh . . . thus preventing his death. Something you would think the captain would be happy about, would you not?"

"Jolly good, a deck of cards in your coat," Roosevelt exclaimed.

"One of three I was carrying," Houdini croaked with an embarrassed smile.

"A secret pocket for hiding cards. A very rum thing to wear on a ship where gentlemen gamble at cards," Captain Railsback chided.

"But *I* do not gamble at cards," Houdini protested. "They are merely professional accessories. Innocent elements of my hanky-panky kit."

"I was unaware that *hanky-panky* could be *innocent*," the captain said.

Nate couldn't help but laugh at that last comment.

Houdini looked in the boy's direction and smiled. "Nate, welcome back to the living!" he cried. "Did I not caution you sternly to let that villain with the gun pass?"

"You did, but how could I? *You* wouldn't have let him by, would you?" Nate challenged.

"Certainly not. But I am older than you. Therefore I am *supposed* to be more foolish. Isn't that right, Wilhelmina, my love?"

"You certainly are the most foolish man I have ever met," Mrs. Houdini said, leaning across the bed to kiss his cheek.

"This 'hanky-panky kit,' Houdini, utterly fascinating," Roosevelt said. "What else do you keep secreted in your clothes?"

"No rabbits or pigeons, sir. I am *not* a magician. Just useful things like cards and string . . . and needles and thread. Lots more."

"Lock picks and keys, right?" the doctor asked. "And files, I'd wager. To get out of handcuffs and chains."

"He doesn't need things like *that*," Nate said.

"Then you know how Houdini makes his escapes?" Roosevelt asked.

"Well, not exactly," Nate said. "It's all a trick, sort of . . . but I know he doesn't cheat."

"Too many words!" Houdini said as loudly as possible under the circumstances. "Allow me to demonstrate."

"There are urgent matters to be discussed. And no time for music hall tomfoolery," insisted Captain Railsback.

"I say, I'll hear none of it," Roosevelt declared. "The man has been shot *and* had his integrity questioned. Let him have his say."

11

In the twinkling of an eye, Houdini transformed himself from incapacitated patient to master of the mysterious. Nate tingled with the electricity of the unexpected. It made him forget how much his head and stomach hurt.

"Doctor, since my clothes are stored away, I will make do with your tools, if you will allow," Houdini said.

"Whatever I can do," the doctor eagerly agreed.

"I need a length of string and as many sewing needles as you can spare. May I borrow some of your surgical equipment?"

"Glad to assist any scientific demonstration," the doctor said as he went to a supply cabinet.

Everyone in the room waited silently; it seemed they

were glad for a momentary diversion. Except for the captain, that is. He groaned noisily a number of times.

"I have more than twenty needles here and as much silk thread as you could possibly need," the doctor offered.

"Twenty is fine—a small demonstration for a small audience. Cut a length of thread several yards long." Houdini sat up in the hospital bed as high as possible. Nate could see the movement caused him some pain.

"I devised this illusion while performing at the Chicago World's Fair in 1893, needing a superior trick to stand apart from the crowd," Houdini explained as he began tying loose knots in the surgical thread. "Keep count, Nate. Stop me at twenty."

"That was six," Nate replied, realizing he already was keeping count.

"I call this the 'East Indian Needles'—wonderfully exotic," Houdini said as his fingers measured and tied at a blinding pace.

"That was twenty knots," Nate said.

Houdini held the thread above his head and handed it to the doctor.

"Since I lost a fair amount of blood this evening, it would be good to get some iron in my system," he said.

Showing everyone the needles in the upturned palm of his hand, Houdini tossed them casually into his mouth. He chewed vigorously, making horrifying sounds. Nate heard metal grating on his teeth and the needles snapping. Mrs. Fuller, the nurse, and the doctor all gasped loudly.

As Houdini finished swallowing, he opened his mouth wide and proudly revealed that all the needles had vanished. Mrs. Houdini handed him a glass of water, which Houdini eagerly drained, smacking his lips afterward.

He took the knotted thread from the doctor and began swallowing it a few inches at a time. By this time, everyone had been drawn in completely, practically hypnotized by Houdini's impromptu performance.

Licking his lips to signal that he was done, Houdini opened his mouth to reveal the end of a piece of the thread still on his tongue, at the back of his throat. Averting his face for an instant, Houdini coughed politely, putting his hand to his mouth, and turned back to the crowd at the foot of his bed.

"Now," he said, "behold a miracle!" He reached inside his mouth and slowly began to pull out the thread. He handed the end to Mrs. Houdini, and she pulled it taut to its full length. The knots all appeared to be the same ones they had seen Houdini tie. But each knot held one of the surgical needles he had swallowed! Somehow, he had threaded the needles into the previously tied knots.

"*Bravo! Bravo!* I say, you *must* come to Oyster Bay sometime—Christmas—and let my family see that jolly trick," the former president cried gleefully.

As the Houdinis thanked Roosevelt for his invitation, the doctor closely examined the thread and needles. "I'll be a . . . I don't know what. It's my silk thread and my needles. Unless you carry a supply of your own, I can't imagine how you did that."

"I said Houdini didn't need to cheat."

"How can you be so sure, Nate?" Houdini asked. "I could have borrowed the thread and needles while the good doctor was removing the bullet. Anything is possible."

"*Very* amusing. *Very* entertaining," the captain said sarcastically as he stepped between Houdini and Roosevelt. "Murder was attempted aboard my ship tonight—a wounded man undergoes surgery nearby as we speak—all very serious business. I will speak privately now with President Roosevelt. The rest of you should retire to your cabins. The evening's excitement is over."

12

It's unlikely that Captain Railsback had ever dealt with so many obstinate passengers at one time. Former President Roosevelt insisted that Houdini—"a man with a nimble mind"—be included in the discussion. Houdini demanded that his wife—"a fount of common sense"—be included. Mrs. Houdini thought that Nate—"a boy with uncommon wisdom for his age, and a victim of the maniac, too"—should be invited to join in, with his mother, naturally.

Having no choice in the matter, the doctor and nurse retired to an office, leaving the door open a crack. The two junior ship's officers backed away and stood guard at the hospital door.

Eager to regain command, the captain sharply questioned Roosevelt.

"Did you expect this attack on your person, sir?"

"An attack on a public person is always a possibility, Captain," the former president acknowledged.

"Is the wounded man your bodyguard?"

"Flanagan was a White House guard until he retired."

"But is he your *personal* bodyguard?"

"You are remarkably curious about my personal arrangements."

"With all respect, your arrangements are no longer personal," the captain said. "Murder has been attempted—"

"*Assassination* is the correct word, I believe," Houdini said, to the captain's obvious annoyance.

"Assassination, then. Either way, under British maritime law, sir, I have the responsibility, and full police powers, to protect the thousands onboard." He paused to let the importance of his position impress his listeners. "Do you expect another attempt on your life?"

"Isn't that better asked of the assailant?" Roosevelt said, deliberately evading the captain's question.

"Answer *this* please: Are you traveling for personal reasons or on matters of state?"

"I cannot be completely candid," Roosevelt said cautiously. "I have no official status; however, I will meet soon with several European heads of state."

"To exchange pleasantries? Shoot pheasant?" The captain was badgering Roosevelt. Nate saw the former president's face begin to flush again, red rising from his neck, and knew that he was about to erupt.

"Blast it, man!" Roosevelt roared. "War clouds are thickening across Europe! A single misstep could plunge the entire world into *war* at any moment. My country wants to prevent that terrible possibility."

In the silence that followed his outburst, Nate questioned whether he had devoted too much of his reading time last summer to crime and Houdini's exploits. *Is the world really so close to war and I just didn't know it?* A glance showed that his mother and Bess beside her were uncomfortable being there in the midst of an argument between men with strong tempers.

"Quite so, a dangerous time," the captain finally conceded. "In general and particular."

It was the particular danger—another attack on Roosevelt's life—that prompted the captain to insist the former president stay in his cabin, under guard, until the ship reached Liverpool. They argued the point vigorously. But Roosevelt abruptly settled the question: "I have never, *never* in my life, run from a fight. I *will not* hide from *cowards* who fire at unarmed men under cover of darkness!" he exclaimed, pounding a clenched fist into the palm of his open hand.

"A complete success!" declared a man's voice from the far end of the ward. As he stepped forward, Nate saw that his collar was undone, his tie missing. Closer up, Nate clearly saw blood spattered across the man's starched white shirt.

"Sir Roland, how is the patient?" asked the captain.

"He should recover nicely—no permanent damage— but a long recuperation is in order. Assuming no infection," the surgeon added.

The ship's doctor popped in. He thanked the famed surgeon profusely, calling it his good fortune that Sir Roland Hanna was aboard. The surgeon noted that Officer Flanagan was the lucky party and dashed away in search of brandy and sandwiches.

The interruption and good news that came with it helped lessen tensions. The captain offered an alternative: seeking guidance from the home office of his shipping line and the American embassy in London. Emergency wireless messages would bring a response by morning. Until that time, Roosevelt agreed to let a guard be posted outside his stateroom. The captain offered to station a guard in the hospital if Houdini felt threatened.

"Nonsense," Houdini said, pressing his wife's hands between his. "The scoundrel may be up for a second attack on Mr. Roosevelt, but surely not on me."

"What about my son? He saw Nate. The gunman *saw* Nate! What if he comes after Nate?" Deborah Fuller's voice quavered with fear. Nate realized that his mother had stayed to ask that terrifying question.

"Calm yourself, madam, your son is not the intended victim." The captain's patronizing tone seemed to irritate both Houdini and Roosevelt. They suggested that silencing a witness might make excellent sense to the would-be assassin. The captain, Roosevelt, and Houdini argued until Nate spoke up.

"But I didn't *really* see him. That is, I saw him well enough to see that he was wearing a disguise."

"Are you certain, Nate?" Houdini pressed. "Nobody wants to take risks with your life."

"I am. I've been going over it, and I'm sure that his mustache and beard were bushy. His sideburns weren't. And the sideburns were a different color from the beard."

"What acute observation, Nate." Houdini beamed.

"But . . . but is that enough?" his mother asked. "What if Nate is wrong?"

"But I am not wrong, Mother. The man also had his hat brim pulled down over his face. He knows that nobody could really see him. It was dark, he was disguised," Nate insisted. "All I could positively recognize again was his overcoat."

In truth, Nate was really telling an enormous lie to calm his mother's fears.

13

It would have been nearly impossible to fall asleep quickly in a strange room with a sore head after all the excitement of the day. As it happened, Nate didn't even need to try. When he and his mother tiptoed into their stateroom, a light turned on immediately. Aunt Alice was sitting bolt upright in her berth. She expected an explanation.

That was no easy task; not a brief one, either. Nate and his mother sat together on the settee made up by a steward as Nate's bed. They took turns describing the chain of events that had occurred in the hours since Deborah Fuller was called away from the ladies' lounge.

Nate had lived with his great-aunt, Mrs. Alice Ludlow,

since his birth, nearly thirteen years before. He could not recall a single time in his entire life when Aunt Alice had listened silently for so long. It was her constant habit to interrupt everyone. Nate felt as if he hardly ever finished a sentence before she corrected his mistake or offered a better opinion.

Now she listened. Occasionally she shook her head or scowled a bit, but she didn't utter a word for more than an hour. When the story was complete up to the moment Nate and his mother had returned to their stateroom, they stopped speaking and waited for her reaction. It was eerily long in coming.

"That man Roosevelt!" she said softly. "Never could mind his own business."

"But, Aunt Alice, he—" Nate began but stopped abruptly when his mother touched a finger to her lips.

"Always playing at things," Mrs. Ludlow continued. "Playing at being a cowboy, a chief of police. A soldier! In *Cuba* of all places."

Nate realized that Roosevelt had triggered thoughts of his father's death in Aunt Alice's mind. His father had been Aunt Alice's favorite, the son she and her husband never had.

"Deborah, death stalks that irresponsible rabble-rouser. I will not lose another nephew to him. Nathaniel, you must not go near him again. Do you understand?"

"But he's in danger, Aunt Alice. And war might break out in Europe any minute."

And I know something that he should know but I don't dare tell you.

"Nathaniel, none of that is *our* concern. This is an omen. We should never have taken this voyage. When we reach Liverpool, we shall not step foot off this ship. We will return home."

"Aunt Alice, we can't do that," Nate protested.

"We can and we shall. And I wish to hear no more about it," she said with finality, flipping the switch of the lamp at her bedside and plunging them into darkness.

"Time for bed," said Nate's mother. "Change in the washroom and I will tuck you in." Leaning over, she whispered, "We will discuss this again, don't fret."

But Nate could not help fretting. He desperately wanted to pull his journal from its hiding place, find the important part, and show it to Houdini. But Houdini was probably sleeping—he had been shot, after all. And Nate didn't want to risk waking Aunt Alice or his mother.

The last thing he remembered before drifting off was wondering where Sir Roland had gone to get sandwiches after operating on Officer Flanagan.

14

Nate had no idea what woke him and no time to think about it. There was enough light seeping through the porthole window curtains to see. He retrieved his journal from where he had stowed it under the settee and recorded his misadventures of the night before. Then it was time to get moving.

After pulling his privacy curtain aside, Nate tiptoed across to the clothes cupboard and opened it. It squeaked loudly. Loudly enough to make him afraid to open another drawer. He wasn't even sure whether his clean underwear was in one of the other drawers. He had been with Mrs. Houdini when his mother unpacked the suitcases.

Nate decided he would just have to wear his pajamas underneath his clothes.

He then grabbed his red leather-bound journal, threw yesterday's clothes over his shoulder, pulled his shoes out from under the settee, and stepped stealthily to the cabin door.

Holding the doorknob, he tried to recall where the nearest public washroom was located. To the left, then the right . . . if he remembered correctly. And certainly no one was on deck this early.

Passing into the predawn light, Nate realized he had been wrong about at least one thing. An elderly man was standing in the alleyway not more than five feet away—looking at his cabin door!

But maybe he wasn't. No sooner had Nate caught sight of him than the man bent to one knee and scoured the floor with his eyes. A frisson of panic passed through Nate.

Could this be the assailant? Looking for me?

Nate stepped nearer the kneeling man. He was dressed in holiday togs: belted tweed jacket, brown trousers, a soft-brimmed cap, and sturdy walking shoes. It couldn't be the gunman in disguise. The man looked to be at least sixty years old. And his short-cropped, gray hair looked very real, not like a disguise.

Then Nate heard the man talking to himself. "Dear me, a half crown. You must be here. I will not leave without you, my precious half crown."

Relieved, Nate offered to help him search.

"That's all right, I've got it," the man declared, holding up a clenched fist. Standing upright with his back toward Nate, the man said, "Ta, must run," and scurried away.

Nate decided that this was going to be a very long trip if he thought everybody he saw was the man trying to kill President Roosevelt.

After dressing, Nate went directly to the hospital on C-deck. Hungrier than the previous night, he was tempted momentarily by the dining room. He took a quick peek through the glass doors, but breakfast wasn't being served yet. Waiters were just laying out place settings and arranging fresh flowers on the tables.

Nate was surprised to find Phin the bellboy and Houdini's dog outside the hospital door. Nate bent over and petted the ever-eager terrier. "Some night, heh, boy? Your master is just fine, though."

Charlie woofed twice.

"Why don't you take him in? Is Houdini sleeping?" Nate asked Charlie's human companion.

"It'd be a blinkin' miracle if 'e is after that snooty mother superior nurse chucked me arse over 'eels," an aggrieved Phin replied.

"The nurse won't let you in?"

"Worried about germs, she says. Barm fly. Gimme the arse-push when I went in. Then I ties up the dog, goes back in, and tries my sweetest to fanny my way round 'er, but she's not 'avin' any."

Charlie raised his head and stared at the bellboy. Nate wondered if the dog was as mystified by Phin's slang as he was.

"I'll tell him you're here, boy," Nate said to Charlie, and stepped inside.

15

Houdini, sitting upright and looking toward the door, seemed to be hoping for a visitor.

"Hail, Nate! Hail the hero of the *Lusitania*! The second we arrive in Liverpool allow me the pleasure of buying you the finest scrapbook available."

"Scrapbook?"

"For your press clippings. Your name will be kept out of the ship's newspaper for your safety. But *soon* you will be hailed as a hero by newspapers across North America and Europe. I will send Marconigrams to my European and American press contacts praising your heroism."

Houdini beckoned Nate to come closer and whispered confidentially: "It is still an open question as to how much newspaper exposure really injures a performer—or a private citizen. And seeing your name, your face, in the papers is certainly a delicious experience."

Nate was taken by the notion that he could become famous.

"I believe Captain Railsback has his work cut out for him," Houdini said thoughtfully. "Finding the proverbial needle in the haystack would be considerably easier than finding this gunman. Consider: there are nearly three thousand people aboard this ship—over two thousand passengers, nearly four hundred stewards and cooks, and belowdecks, hundreds of men shoveling coal to fuel the turbine engines. Even if we count only men, that still leaves *thousands* of suspects. A nearly impossible task."

"Not if we know who he is," Nate said triumphantly.

"But we do not know . . . do we?"

"I do!"

"You said all you could recognize was his overcoat."

"That was . . . being truthful . . . an untruth."

"I must hear more," Houdini said.

Nate told him about the observation exercise he had done before sailing and how he was positive that the overcoat the gunman wore was the same coat one of his "maybes" had worn on the pier. Then Nate read his description of the man from his journal. "Tall, young, thin with thinning hair. Walk undistinguished. <u>Circular purple birthmark (wart?) on left nostril.</u> Very agitated—always in motion. Wears overcoat (no hat!) even though warm and sunny for October."

"How *positive* are you that the man on the pier and the assassin are the same man?" Houdini asked.

"*Absolutely* positive!" Nate replied firmly.

"Even though, from the brief look I got, they seem very dissimilar. The gunman had a beard and . . ."

"Theatrical makeup," Nate said.

Houdini pounded the blankets on his bed and said: "By George! As former president Roosevelt likes to say. Nate, you are amazing." Houdini ran the fingers of both hands through his wiry hair and looked up, saying: "I must think a moment."

After a few moments, though, a great bustle of activity interrupted them. Looking past Nate toward the front door, Houdini hailed two of the several visitors entering the ward: "Mr. President, Captain, how are you this morning?" Then, looking toward Nate, he whispered: "Not a word of what you know to anyone, not yet. Put your book away."

Nate was puzzled and a bit disappointed, but he followed Houdini's instructions without hesitation.

"You sound bully!" Roosevelt stepped around Nate and shook Houdini's hand energetically. The captain and two junior officers positioned themselves at the foot of Houdini's bed.

"Not too much the worse for wear," Houdini said.

"Jolly good. Now, I must see my friend Flanagan. Where is he?"

"Follow me, sir," said a starchy nurse. She had rushed into the ward intent on "shushing" the noisy visitors but had decided against it when she realized the offenders were the ship's captain and a former president of the United States. "Officer Flanagan is under twenty-four-hour care in the surgery, so as not to disturb our other patient."

Wishing Houdini a speedy recovery, Roosevelt departed.

After he was out of earshot, Captain Railsback addressed Houdini. "Good morning," he said gruffly, hands thrust in his pockets. "I trust that you are well cared for. Is there anything special my staff can do for you?"

"You could get me to solid land."

"We are doing that, sir: faster, more smoothly, and more comfortably than *any* other ship plying these waters."

"Immediately is never soon enough. I travel uncomfortably on water, even without the unexpected hole in my side."

"You would be more comfortable in saloon class, in one of our suites. A sitting room and private bath make all the difference in the world," the captain said.

"It's just as luxurious to be seasick in second class, and a darn sight cheaper, too," Houdini countered.

"Not on this voyage, Mr. Houdini. Allow me to move

you to a suite on B-deck, compliments of the management."

A grin spread across Houdini's face. "Nate, which old saw applies? Am I looking the gift horse in the mouth or testing for the strings attached?"

Nate could tell that the captain was one of those adults who believed that children should be seen and never heard. Grinning like Houdini, he said, "I think Mrs. Houdini would enjoy a suite. And it would be nearer our cabin."

"I will be frank," Captain Railsback said, ignoring Nate and trying to bury his hands even deeper in his coat pockets. "The line's managers directed me to move you and your wife to a suite from which you could supervise your investigation."

"*My* investigation?"

"Yes, sir. I am required to request that you assume responsibility for *both* the protection of Mr. Roosevelt and the capture of his assailant."

"This is unexpected," Houdini said.

"And highly irregular," Railsback said. "It is *disagreeable* to cede authority to a passenger, but those are my orders. Direct from our London headquarters."

"Curious" was Houdini's only reply.

"Our managing director contacted New Scotland Yard," the captain explained. "When Superintendent Thompson heard that you were onboard, he strongly urged this course of action."

"Good old Thompson. I've shown him a thing or two in the past—breaking out of his lockup, suggesting the whereabouts of several wanted criminals, and the like. But I had no thought the superintendent had *such* a high opinion of me," Houdini said with unmistakable enjoyment.

"I merely obey the orders handed down by my superiors."

"I accept the responsibility," Houdini said gravely. "It is no less than my patriotic duty."

"I will put four junior officers at your disposal."

"They may be helpful to some extent."

"My officers are brave, loyal, and intelligent, sir, and—"

"And they are in uniform, Captain. Useful to keep the killer away from Mr. Roosevelt, not to flush him out and capture him."

"Mr. Roosevelt is still uncooperative," the captain said. "He wants no guard. He refuses to remain in his stateroom."

"An independent man," Houdini said.

"A cowboy," the captain sneered to himself. Turning to Houdini, he asked: "What's next?"

"Getting dressed and out of here is the first thing. I need a suit of clothes not stained with blood. Nate, is that bellboy Newborn outside?"

"He was when I came in."

"Then be so good as to tell him to return Charlie to the care of my beloved wife while he organizes a party to move us to . . . the cabin number, Captain?"

"B-72."

"Newborn will organize our move to B-72 and then re-turn with fresh clothing for me."

"I could do that . . . fetch fresh clothes for you," Nate said.

Houdini looked closely at him for a second, as if making a difficult calculation. "Agreed. Get the wheels of progress turning, my friend."

As Nate hurried out, he heard Houdini tell the captain that he wished to discuss the former president's eyesight.

Nate saw that the morning had dawned sunny and clear. The crisp air had a salty tang. Through his feet, Nate could feel the constant vibration of the engines far below, churning away as the ship plowed toward England. Using his hand as a visor, he looked left and right before sighting Phin and Charlie in the distance, near the deck railing.

The deck had constant foot traffic from passengers entering and leaving the first-class dining room. Breakfast was now in full sway. Enticing smells were carried by the breeze that was always brisk, Nate guessed, on a moving ocean liner.

Approaching Phin and Charlie, Nate saw another person with them. A man he thought he recognized. But the sun was behind them, making it difficult to see. Nate blinked and rubbed his eyes, and suddenly the bellboy and dog were by themselves again.

"Were you just speaking with someone?" Nate asked.

"I was."

"Who was he? What's his name?"

"Lord love a duck! You think I know the name of ev'ry blinkin' passenger?"

"No, of course not. Was he wearing a belted tweed jacket and soft cap?"

"Ain't that what 'alf the men 'ere is wearin'?" Phin asked, grandly waving his free arm to point out the accuracy of his statement. Nate laughed in agreement.

"Was he about sixty years old, with short gray hair?"

Phin thought and nodded in agreement.

" 'E was."

"I wish that I knew who he was exactly," Nate said. Then, wondering if he wasn't getting too suspicious, he dropped the subject. He told Phin the plan and let the bellboy and Charlie lead him toward the Houdinis' cabin.

"I took 'im for a crusher," Phin said unexpectedly.

"A crusher?" Nate repeated, uncomprehending.

"Yeah, a rozzer. 'Ad bluebottle shoes, 'e did."

"A policeman? You think he's a policeman?"

"Aye, that's what I think," Phin said with satisfaction.

Far from it, Nate thought. *Keep your eyes peeled from now on,* he warned himself.

16

Nate practically ran back to the hospital. He was trying to keep pace with Mrs. Houdini, a woman eager to see her injured husband. When they arrived, Houdini—barefoot in a long, woolen gown—was testing a cane for the doctor and the starchy nurse.

"Nothing to it," Houdini said.

"I would prefer that you stay in hospital one more day at the least," the doctor advised.

"Doctor, the man's own brother is a physician. Do you think Houdini has ever listened to him?" Mrs. Houdini walked over, kissed her husband amiably on the cheek, and transferred the fresh clothing to his free arm. "*Ach!* I have seen him do worse to himself. It is only a scratch."

"Who am I to argue with a man who can thread needles in his throat?" the doctor asked.

"How *did* you do that?" Nate asked. "In a hospital gown, without your hanky-panky kit?"

"Nate, you really believe he needs props?" Mrs. Houdini laughed. "I remember him doing the needles trick naked once. Naked, in a locked jail cell after being *thoroughly* examined by several doctors."

"Good thing you did not attempt that on my ward," said the nurse. "No pets, no loud talk, no nudity here. Please dress behind this screen."

While Houdini dressed, Nate and Mrs. Houdini visited the now conscious Officer Flanagan. The wounded bodyguard much regretted that he was unable to do his job, protecting the former president.

To comfort him, Mrs. Houdini said, "My husband will do his utmost, as will the crew, to keep Mr. Roosevelt safe. Your job is recuperating."

Nate nearly burst from wanting to blurt out how close they were—because of his secret information—to catching the gunman. But Houdini had said to tell no one, and Nate reasoned that, even if that prohibition did not include Mrs. Houdini, it did include Officer Flanagan.

Returning to the ward, they found Houdini dressed and raring to go.

"Wilhelmina, my dear, have you had breakfast?" Houdini asked.

"Coffee and toast, but I *could* eat."

"I am thinking that Nate and I should discuss matters privately over breakfast, if you do not mind."

"*Ach*, I have hours of unpacking to do. I will ask Deborah to keep me company."

"I think you would have to include Aunt Alice, too," Nate suggested sheepishly.

"Why would I not? I find your great-aunt delightful company. You men go off by yourselves . . . But what about President Roosevelt?"

"He is sharing the officers' mess—what a phrase! I am sure that the food is even better there than in the dining room," Houdini said.

They parted company with Mrs. Houdini at the door. Her final words to Nate, whispered behind her husband's back, were "If he turns pale . . . or begins to bleed, send for me immediately."

Food at last, Nate told himself as he made the short trip to the dining room with Houdini. He was practically giddy—from hunger and from the notion that he was going to identify and capture the man who had tried to assassinate Theodore Roosevelt.

Inside, Houdini eased himself into an elegant, cushioned dining chair. Nate couldn't resist spinning his in a circle, easy enough to do since all the chairs were anchored by steel posts coming up from the floor. Nate had seen that practically everything—chairs, tables, sofas—was anchored to keep it steady when seas were rough.

"Tackle your food this morning, Nate. You need your strength and your wits," Houdini said.

The sheer spectacle of dining had dazzled Nate the previous evening. He had been too distracted to pay much attention to the food. Now he studied the breakfast menu as if it were a passage in Latin he had been asked to explain to the class:

SALOON CLASS—WEDNESDAY, OCTOBER 11TH, 1911

-BREAKFAST-

BAKED APPLES—FRUIT—STEAMED PRUNES
QUAKER OATS—BROILED HOMINY—PUFFED RICE
FRESH HERRING
FINDON HADDOCK—SMOKED SALMON
GRILLED MUTTON—KIDNEYS & BACON
GRILLED HAM—GRILLED SAUSAGE
LAMB CALLOPS—VEGETABLE STEW
FRIED, SHIRRED, POACHED & BOILED EGGS
PLAIN & TOMATO OMELETTES TO ORDER
SIRLOIN STEAK & MUTTON CHOPS TO ORDER
MASHED SAUTÉ AND JACKET POTATOES
COLD MEAT
VIENNA AND GRAHAM ROLLS
SODA & SULTANA SCONES—CORN BREAD
BUCKWHEAT CAKES

BLACK CURRANT CONSERVE — NARBONNE HONEY
OXFORD MARMALADE
WATERCRESS

"I think I'd like fried eggs with Vienna rolls. And grilled mutton. Grilled sausage, too," Nate finally said.

"Bring that for my colleague," Houdini told the waiter. "For me, only fruit and water with ice chips and lemon."

"But that's practically nothing. You can't live on fruit and water for five days!" Nate declared.

"I've survived longer on less. And better safe than sorry. The sea is calm and the voyage is remarkably smooth . . . so far. Who knows what may happen tomorrow?"

"Do you really get so terribly seasick?"

"I do! I am not even a fair-weather sailor."

"But you're an aviator, the first person to fly in Australia," Nate said, remembering a clipping from Houdini's scrapbooks.

"It was only a short flight, but the first."

"Flying doesn't make you sick? Or scared?"

"Never sick or fearful. In the air, all the tension and strain leave me. But the steamer trip back was another matter. I was ill the whole voyage."

"Maybe you could hypnotize yourself into thinking that the *Lusitania* is actually an airplane," Nate said.

"No, I am a terrible liar."

"But if you're sick on this voyage, someone might die," Nate said.

"So much responsibility, so little help."

"The captain offered four of his junior officers."

"Naval officers will make excellent guards but horrible detectives. Naval officers give and take orders without room for discussion. Detectives ask questions. They listen, they observe, they try to separate truth from lies. No, the workday routine of Captain Railsback and his men makes them highly unsuitable for detective work."

"But there's really no detective work needed!" Nate said.

"Because you can recognize the gunman without his disguise?"

"That's right!"

"And a quick toss of the thousands onboard will expose him because he has no backup disguise?"

"Oh, I hadn't thought of a second disguise."

"He may not have one. But this is so tedious, calling him 'he' or 'the gunman.' 'He' needs a name."

"What sort of name? We have no idea who 'he' really is," Nate said.

"We know enough. You cunningly observed that he is a highly agitated, nervous individual—a Nervous Nellie or Nervous Ned. What do you think of plain Ned?"

After pondering a bit, Nate said: "I don't like it. Old Ned Phillips taught me to fish. But anyway, I think he was more of a Jumpy Jack than a Nervous Ned."

"Jumpy it is then. Just Jumpy." They agreed with a handshake as the waiter brought breakfast. Houdini silently peeled a banana, cut it into tiny sections with knife and fork, and nibbled slowly, giving Nate the opportunity to devour his eggs and grilled meat. After the boy pushed aside his empty plate, Houdini ordered a pitcher of milk for Nate and more ice water for himself.

Nate drank two glasses rapidly, wiped his lips with a napkin, and was about to ask a question when Houdini suggested that they retire to a more private place.

17

The "more private place" Houdini had in mind was the first-class writing room and library on A-deck. The room was nearly empty at this early hour of the day. Men conducting business were next door, dictating letters to typewriting ladies. Other passengers digesting breakfast were enjoying pipes and cigars in the smoking lounge nearby. In the library only two solitary passengers were visible as Houdini picked comfortable wing chairs in a corner near the windows.

"Why are we being so secretive?" Nate asked.

"To protect your life, of course," Houdini replied coolly.

"So . . . you think I'm in danger?"

"Not as long as *we* are the only people who know about Jumpy's purple wart. *We are,* are we not?"

"You said tell no one, so I didn't; not even Mrs. Houdini."

"Good. On a ship, gossip and rumor spread so quickly. A waiter overhears and innocently tells another. Soon the kitchen knows. Then the whole ship."

"But we do have to tell the captain, so his men will know who to search for."

"Let us weigh the alternatives. The captain cannot search cabin to cabin—an Englishman's home is his castle, after all. And unless Jumpy happened to be in one of the very first cabins to be searched, a search would be futile. Word of it would spread too quickly. All incriminating evidence would go into the sea."

"But if we caught him, why would we need evidence? I was an eyewitness," protested Nate.

"An eyewitness to a shooting, yes. A shooting by a bearded man you *think* wore a false nose to hide a telltale facial feature."

Nate let it sink in and agreed finally.

"I couldn't swear beyond any doubt, under oath, that the man on Pier 54 was Jumpy . . . even though I'm sure of it."

"So we must catch him in the act or catch him with the evidence or, best of all, prevent another attempt and watch Mr. Roosevelt leave the ship unharmed." Houdini leaned toward Nate. "After all, neither of us is a policeman. I do not wish you to be in harm's way."

A passenger who had entered minutes earlier finally selected a book from the shelves at the opposite end of the library. He scanned the room and chose a seat inches from Houdini and Nate.

"I say," the reader addressed them, "one never can read outdoors on a ship—too much sun, too much wind, what?"

Nate tried to size him up as Houdini cheerily agreed: "Just my thought that—too much, entirely."

"That's it, then," the middle-aged Englishman agreed. He did a double take and asked breathlessly: "You're not Harry Houdini, are you? The magician?"

"I *am* Houdini—Mystic Entertainer, Psychic Investigator, Master Mystifier—at your service."

"Oh, that is magnificent. My wife and I have seen you many times. Rum luck she's not here. She will never believe I met you."

"But she will," Houdini said as he reached inside his jacket's breast pocket. "What is your charming wife's name, sir?"

"Her name is Faith."

Houdini scratched a message in pencil on the business card he'd retrieved from his jacket, pushed himself up from the plush chair, and handed the man his autographed card.

"Must exercise now; doctor's orders. Good meeting you." Houdini limped hastily toward the exit.

"We may have more privacy in a crowd, Nate, if we keep moving," he said to his young companion. "Drat, I do wish Bess had brought my slouch hat. Nobody recognizes me wearing that."

The A-deck promenade was too crowded for Houdini's taste. Couples ambled arm in arm, the women shielding themselves from the sun with parasols. Some leaned over the railings to watch the sea rolling past. Dozens pursued various activities—reading, knitting, chatting—in the comfort of deck chairs.

"Let's try B-deck," Houdini said, taking the stairway down. Nate noticed that Houdini's walk was labored and—judging by his friend's occasional winces—painful, but the boy said nothing. *What can I say or do that would help? Nothing!*

"I was surprised that you returned the magic books I sent last summer," Houdini said suddenly. "Even more so that you asked for books about crime instead. Most boys your age are fascinated by magic."

"They were beautiful books, but . . . I don't think I could ever be a very good magician. *You* aren't a magician," Nate answered.

"My wife, my agent, now you—nobody considers me a magician!"

"But you don't *call* yourself a magician, that's what I

meant. I just think solving crime is more up my alley. Making a contribution to society, that's what I mean."

"Doesn't my work as an entertainer make a contribution to society, Nate? Is there really anything greater than making people forget their worries?"

Nate searched for words. He hadn't intended to insult Houdini.

"Of course there is. Saving a life, for example," Houdini said in answer to his own question.

"So what can we do?" Nate asked, grateful that his friend wasn't offended. "Something that wouldn't be risky, so you won't be worried about me."

"What would that be, Nate? We know so little," Houdini said as they strolled sternward on the nearly empty promenade. "Is Jumpy a solitary lunatic with a grudge? Is he a dedicated terrorist—an anarchist or the like—who will stop at nothing to finish his mission? Does he have an accomplice, someone who will take over if he is captured?"

"Darn! We don't even know whether he is a passenger or a crew member," Nate said. "Catching Jumpy isn't going to be easy, even with what I know."

"That is why we must keep what you know—valuable as it is—strictly secret. Until we determine a way to use it without putting you at risk."

"So the plan is to prevent Jumpy from striking again rather than hunt him down?"

"Yes."

Nate had expected more than that for an answer. He had expected Houdini to lay out the plan.

"How can we make a plan?" Houdini asked. He had a scary way of knowing what a person was thinking. "We cannot formulate a plan until we consider everything we actually know. Tell me everything you know about Jumpy, Nate, based upon your observations."

Nate described Jumpy physically—in disguise and out. He described the gunman's mannerisms, the way in which he stalked and shot at Roosevelt, the way in which he escaped.

"Now, make deductions—predictions—about his future behavior based on his past actions," Houdini instructed.

Nate fretted. He wanted to come up with the right solution.

"Take your time, Nate." Houdini leaned against the railing and stared at the ocean rolling swiftly by. At twenty-five knots per hour, even a ship as large as the *Lusitania* seemed to be moving very fast.

"All right . . . He didn't get as close to Mr. Roosevelt as he could have, to make sure that he killed him. Then he fled after shooting you. So we know that he feared being caught. He wanted to kill the man and get away with it."

"Superb," Houdini said. "He is not a martyr. And that tells us . . ."

"That if he tries again, it will be in similar circumstances."

"So we should expect . . ."

"That he will attack at night. In disguise. And with a planned escape route," Nate said, striking his open palm with his fist three times.

"*Bravo!* It is safe to assume that is all true. And will change only if Jumpy does not get the opportunity he wants. Then he may panic and start shooting in broad daylight, desperate to accomplish his 'mission.' But that should not happen before the end of the voyage. Do you agree?"

"I do," Nate said. "And that means we just have to make it impossible for Jumpy to get near Mr. Roosevelt unguarded."

"Which could be as easy as making an elephant disappear."

18

To protect the former president, Houdini and Nate needed his cooperation. A genial junior officer informed them that Roosevelt had been on the navigating bridge with Captain Railsback minutes earlier.

"Not on the best of terms, are they?" the officer added with a smile.

Walking to the bow, Nate saw that the navigating bridge was the highest inhabitable area of the ship. The funnels that continuously vented smoke rose considerably higher. Nate had pictured a bridge based on nautical stories he had read but realized that those images were old-fashioned. He knew the ship was not being steered by a ragged sailor spinning a gigantic wooden wheel. That made Nate more eager to see how it was actually done.

"Welcome to the bridge, gentlemen," said the uniformed officer who ushered them in. "I am Mr. Clyde, the *Lusitania*'s navigational officer. I presume that you are here to see Mr. Roosevelt."

"He is here?" Houdini asked.

"In the smoking room, sir."

"And the captain?"

"The captain is in the wireless room. Quite a bit of message traffic today," Mr. Clyde said.

Nate scanned the room filled with incomprehensible machinery. At the front, a wall of windows curving outward gave a wide view of the sea ahead. Brass gauges on pedestals ringed the front wall, their markings mysterious to a landlubber.

To the right was the wheelhouse—a floor-to-ceiling mahogany box. A door was cracked open, and inside Nate could see a complex set of gears turning slightly.

"Nate and I would appreciate a guided tour," Houdini said, again reading Nate's private thoughts. "For now, alas, duty calls. Could you take us to Mr. Roosevelt?"

"This way, sir. And you both have a standing offer—there's nothing I enjoy more than showing *Lucy* off," Mr. Clyde said.

Roosevelt was seated at an ample round table, a coffee cup in one hand and what appeared to be a long telegraph message in the other. A number of similar papers were piled at his elbow. Hearing them enter the room, the former president looked up and squinted through his pince-nez spectacles. "Is that you, Houdini? And young Nate with you?"

"Good day to you, Mr. President," Houdini replied formally.

Roosevelt rose to shake Houdini's hand. "No need for formality, since it appears we are yoked together," he said, referring to the papers. "You are just Houdini. I am plain Colonel. Agreed?"

"Agreed, Colonel," Houdini replied.

"The same applies for you, young man."

"Yes, sir, Colonel," Nate said.

He observed that both men were cut from the same mold physically. Taller than Houdini by four or five inches, Roosevelt also had a massive chest and powerful, muscular arms. He appeared amazingly fit considering that he must have been nearly twenty years older than Houdini.

Both were famously devoted to physical activity, what Roosevelt called "the strenuous life." For the colonel that meant swimming, boxing, tennis, and hunting. Houdini's strenuous activities were more practically oriented. He didn't swim, but Nate knew that Houdini frequently submerged himself for long periods in ice water—part of the training regimen of a man who jumped from bridges into frigid rivers.

Grabbing the pile of papers from the table, the colonel

angrily said, "Our secretary of state and his British counterpart doubt my ability to take care of myself. They make me out to be practically helpless."

"Caution is like cod-liver oil, Colonel. A healthy dose is often prudent no matter how distasteful it is."

"Perfectly diplomatic," Roosevelt said, baring his teeth in a grin known around the world. "But it's all a tempest in a teakettle."

"Because all the protection you require is that long-barreled Navy pistol holstered inside your coat?"

"Who told you I carry a Colt, Houdini?"

Looking closely, Nate could see a bulge under the colonel's left shoulder.

"My eyes are my only spies, Colonel. I avoid more costly sources of information."

"What a perfect corker you are, Houdini."

"You cannot deny that it would be an unspeakable disaster for an ex-president of the United States to be assassinated on this ship—more of a disaster for the King of England than it would be for you."

"More of a disaster for the king?"

"The king will suffer all the criticism if you arrive in Liverpool dead. You will not have to listen to any of it, even if it is entirely your doing."

Roosevelt could not argue with Houdini's logic. Instead, he launched into a long recitation of his triumphs over deadly danger—as a rancher in the Wild West, as a police commissioner, as the colonel of a regiment that fought for the liberation of Cuba from Spain.

The mention of Cuba unleashed all the thoughts roiling around in the back of Nate's mind since he'd first laid eyes on Roosevelt. He didn't really know how he felt about the Hero of San Juan Hill. Aunt Alice clearly detested Roosevelt, blaming him for the death of Nate's father. Nate didn't know if his mother felt the same.

He did know that he would like to talk with Roosevelt about his father. To ask him what his father was like. Nate's mother and great-aunt dearly loved the man, but what did his commanding officer—a man among men, a man like Houdini—think of him?

But Nate knew this was not the time to ask.

"These goody-goody measures are utterly pointless," Roosevelt said. "*If* the assassin tries again, I am forewarned and armed. If he comes from the *front*, my reflexes and strength will defeat him. If he fires from *behind*, I will be dead—"

"Your courage is enviable, Colonel," Houdini said, interrupting Roosevelt's lecture. "Your eyesight is not."

"What the blazes are you implying?"

"Last evening I observed that you had some difficulties," Houdini said very meekly.

Nate remembered observing the same thing. When Jumpy was pointing a gun at him, it had seemed as if Roosevelt couldn't see it.

"A steward sent wireless messages to several reporters I know in Washington," Houdini continued. "They replied that your vision has been *diminished* ever since you were injured during a White House boxing session."

"Damn and blast! They should have more respect for my privacy. Who told you that, Houdini?"

"Does it matter? The point is that you really cannot defend yourself as well as you once could."

Roosevelt sat and thought. Houdini dropped heavily onto a chair.

His wound is worse than he lets on, Nate thought. *Keep that in mind.*

"Would you put me under house arrest, Houdini? That's what the captain intensely desires—to make me a prisoner."

"I would like you on your guard if not under guard."

At this point the captain arrived, and the discussion heated up again. Roosevelt was reluctant, the captain was insistent, Houdini was conciliatory, and Nate was silent.

A flash of inspiration broke across Houdini's face like dawn breaking after a dark, stormy night. "Let's amuse ourselves," he suggested brightly. Grabbing everyone's attention, he continued: "If I suggested cutting cards to see who prevails, I wager neither of you would agree to it."

Roosevelt and Captain Railsback vigorously agreed.

"But, Colonel, last evening you voiced a fascination with telepathy. Let's say I demonstrate that I am telepathic. If I convince you I have extrasensory powers, will you believe you are in danger? That is, if I have sensed it telepathically?"

"I've taken a shine to you, Houdini, but you won't paint me into a corner that way. You're too cunning to accept at face value."

"Understood. But a little mind reading will be more diverting than this discussion. We can argue later."

19

Listening to Houdini's orders, Nate appreciated how cunning his mentor was. Houdini suggested that while he and Roosevelt strolled to the first-class lounge, the colonel could invite any passengers he chose to be part of the demonstration. That would certainly eliminate any possibility of colluding with a secret assistant, Houdini said. He requested that two officers accompany them—to move furniture and create a stage. That left the captain free to return to his pressing duties.

"This mind joining can't proceed without my psychic partner, Mrs. Houdini. Nate, would you ask her to join us in the lounge? And please invite your mother and aunt. They may find it amusing."

Nate knew that his mother would love to attend, but he wasn't at all sure about Aunt Alice. Even though Nate and Houdini had saved her life, she remained vaguely resentful of Houdini—as if he had caused the problem, not solved it. And the way she felt about Roosevelt!

Nate was game, though. He raced out of the bridge and down the narrow iron staircase toward the A-deck.

It's him again!

Seeing a familiar man out of the corner of his eye, Nate stopped halfway down the stairs and clenched the iron rails tightly. He was sure it was the man he'd first seen looking for a coin on the deck outside his cabin.

This is the third time I've seen him today. Is he Jumpy's partner? Or his boss?

Nate would have sworn the man was looking up toward the bridge when he caught sight of him, but at second glance, the gray-haired man in a soft cap was turned in the opposite direction. He was hailing a strolling couple, walking toward them and talking like an old friend.

Eager to hear what he was saying, Nate scrambled down the stairs and walked past the threesome.

"I am certain of it. We met at the Newmarket races. Of course, you would probably remember my wife better than me," the soft-capped man was saying.

Nate desperately wanted to turn and see if the couple actually recognized the man but knew he couldn't risk it. He decided that, whoever he was, the elderly man was no threat to Roosevelt in broad daylight on the crowded promenade, so he carefully threaded his way through the throngs toward the Houdinis' new stateroom.

Phin answered his knock. "Join the party, mate—er, sir," he said in greeting.

It was a party indeed. Nate's mother and great-aunt were in the spacious sitting room with Mrs. Houdini.

"One of our missing escorts has turned up at last," Mrs. Houdini said.

"Did I miss something?" Nate asked as he bent over and kissed both his mother and great-aunt on their cheeks.

"You missed lunching with us. And we missed lunching with you," his mother said.

"You must eat at regular times, Nathaniel," his great-aunt sternly added. "If you do not, it will shorten your life as surely as whiskey or cigars."

Aunt Alice had a never-ending list of things and activities that were sure to shorten life. Nate regretted missing lunch. He wondered how he had failed to notice.

"A young man can have no better example of clean living than my husband, let me assure you, Mrs. Ludlow. Houdini doesn't smoke or drink or swear. Clean living is his watchword."

That reassurance yielded only a skeptical "Hmmm" from the elderly woman.

"I'm sure that I can get some sandwiches later, after the exhibition Houdini is putting on for Colonel Roosevelt in the lounge. That's why I'm here, to invite you," said Nate.

"How exciting," said Nate's mother. "What sort of exhibition will it be, Nate?"

"Mind reading."

"Mind reading!" repeated Mrs. Houdini, clearly alarmed.

"Your husband actually reads minds, Mrs. Houdini?" asked Aunt Alice.

"If he says so, I suppose he can," she replied cautiously.

"Let me take your arm, Aunt Alice. Yours, too, Mother," Nate offered. He was surprised that his aunt, having been cruelly fooled by a phony medium, was still eager to believe in psychic phenomena.

"Is this going to be spooky, Nate?" his mother asked.

"Houdini said it will be amusing," Nate answered.

"We will see, won't we?" Mrs. Houdini said. "Phin, since Charlie is sleeping soundly in the bedroom, please escort me to this amusing exhibition."

Nate felt a reluctance in Mrs. Houdini that he couldn't fathom. He decided to ignore it. After all, he had just convinced three adults to participate in something he thought would be great fun. That was accomplishment enough.

20

Walking the short distance to the lounge was another—totally unexpected—accomplishment. In the brief time Nate had been in the suite, weather conditions had changed drastically. The pleasant breeze had given way to driving winds. Gray, rain-filled clouds hid the sun.

The grand promenade was practically deserted. Deck chair blankets, abandoned by fleeing sun lovers, snapped in the wind. Many passengers had run for cover in the lounge Houdini had chosen because it would be uncrowded and safe.

Hooking their arms together and leaning into the wind, Nate and his companions finally entered a room filled with curious passengers. Houdini called and waved, urging them to come forward.

More than a dozen sofas ringed the wood-paneled walls. Dozens of overstuffed easy chairs were scattered through the room, as were small round tables with matching armchairs. Practically every seat was occupied. A few passengers stared out the windows, hoping the weather would change for the better as rapidly as it had turned for the worse. But nearly all eyes were glued to the front of the room, where something exciting was about to unfold.

Because most of the room's tables and chairs were bolted to the floor—as was the furniture in the dining room—Houdini had decided to use a heavy sofa as his stage. The ship's officers had moved one to an open area at one end of the room and turned it toward the wall. A dozen movable easy chairs faced the sofa in theater style—two rows of six chairs lined up for the Fuller-Ludlow family and Colonel Roosevelt's invited guests, the Lynches.

It was a merry group, except for Aunt Alice. When introduced to Roosevelt, she was distinctly frosty.

"I say, dear lady, does this telepathy demonstration disturb your sensibility?" the former president asked sympathetically.

"A genuine display of psychic powers would be most welcome. It is your presence that disturbs me, sir," she said bitterly.

Taken aback, Roosevelt jokingly asked, "Are you a Democrat, madam? Have I disappointed you politically?"

"You are responsible for my nephew's death," she answered, eyes fixed on him. "You caused the death of this boy's father, sir."

Roosevelt flushed. He looked toward Nate. Nate's mother seemed frozen. The Lynches coughed uncomfortably and looked at their shoes.

"No comedy, please. I cannot *bear* comedy in my act," Houdini said loudly. "You've had your little joke, Mrs. Ludlow. Would you and Deborah take a seat? We can continue this later."

Before the unpleasantness could go any further, Houdini projected his stage voice to the back of the room: "Layyy-deees and Genn-tell-mennn!" Moving behind the sofa, he continued: "Pul-leeeze give me your *un-divided* attention. *The Magical, Mystifying Houdinis*, acclaimed by millions on four continents, including *Australia*, have brought their mind-twisting, reason-defying powers to the *Lusitania* lounge this afternoon to honor and entertain the world's *greatest* statesman, diplomat, outdoorsman, and author—President Theodore Roosevelt."

Roosevelt grinned widely and waved as the audience applauded enthusiastically. He took the chair farthest away from Aunt Alice.

"Will the two persons chosen by Colonel Roosevelt—people who are certain that they have never met me before today—come forward to assist?"

The Lynches edged their way around Aunt Alice and stood near Houdini.

It was the couple he'd seen talking with the man who'd been following them, Nate realized.

I should have slowed down and listened to them without drawing attention to myself. Could "Newmarket races" be code? Darn, is Jumpy here?

Nate tried to scan the crowded room inconspicuously.

"Three questions: Your names, if you please."

"I'm Jackie Lynch and this is my wife, Rosemary."

"Second: Do either of you know me, Houdini?"

"We've seen your show in the vaudeville. Does that count?" the young man asked, prompting some laughter in the crowd.

"It proves that you have excellent taste. What I meant was this: Have I ever spoken with either you or your enchanting wife before being introduced by Colonel Roosevelt moments ago? Have we ever exchanged letters? Or visited each other's homes?"

Mr. and Mrs. Lynch shook their heads gravely from side to side, answering no to each question.

"Excellent. My final question: Does each of you have a handkerchief you would lend for this demonstration?"

"That we do. Clean ones, too!" Jackie Lynch said.

"We're in business then," Houdini said.

Nate observed that the young couple were not typical first-class passengers. Mr. Lynch wore a green-and-red checked suit, the kind with a giant fabric belt. Nate thought that such a vividly colored suit might be normal onboard a ship, but it certainly did not go with the man's blue-banded fedora hat. Nate had learned that much about style during his summer stint at Bennett & Son, Gentlemen's Hatters.

Nate didn't know much about women's clothing, but he knew that Mrs. Lynch's outfit was more colorful than anything he had seen his mother wear.

They were odd ducks, out of place on this deck, he concluded.

Houdini excused himself to the audience and conferred privately with the young couple. Facing the audience once more, he loudly resumed: "Lay-dees and Gen-tell-men, we have the pleasure of being assisted today by Mr. and Mrs. Jackie Lynch. Jackie *was* a New York sanitation department employee. He and his bride are going home to claim his inheritance—an *estate* in County Meath, Ireland. Is that right?"

"Yes, it is. In Kells, County Meath. But Ireland is not my home. It was my parents' home. And my uncle's . . . who left me the estate."

"And the estate has horses?"

"Yes, it does," Mr. Lynch proudly said. "As well as sheep and cattle and pigs. Dogs, too!"

"Bully!" said the colonel. "There is no better life than the outdoor life."

"This will be quite a change in life, from cleaning the streets of New York to owning a horse farm. You could say that from now on"—Houdini paused dramatically, looking toward the audience—"the muck will be on the other foot, yes?"

"So it will, so it will. You won't catch me chasing near the *back* end of horses anymore."

This last exchange got the entire crowd, except for Nate, laughing. *Is that actually who the man is?* he asked himself.

When the laughter subsided, Houdini sat on the sofa, his back to the audience, and asked the Lynches to blindfold him using both of their clean handkerchiefs. When they were sure that "no man could see through those blinkers," a claim that Nate felt certain was untrue, Houdini asked the Lynches to observe him closely.

"Make sure that I have no hand mirror I can use to look backward, no way to see what is happening behind my back. Bess, when you are ready, please proceed."

"Ready when you are, Houdini," his wife said in a theatrical voice. She walked toward the rear of the room, paused in front of an elderly man, and touched her hand to his shoulder.

"Before proceeding, I beg the audience's indulgence and ask for absolute silence," Mrs. Houdini said. "The communication between Houdini and myself must be complete. That is extremely difficult to achieve, so *pray* be as quiet as possible. Now, Houdini, concentrate. Concentrate well. I have my hand on a member of the audience. Tell me that person's age."

"I would say that the gentleman you stand next to looks marvelously young for his age but is well past seventy years."

"My stars, you're right. I was seventy-three last month," the man said.

"Houdini, you are not concentrating hard enough," Bess scolded. "Seventy-three is hardly 'well past seventy.' Let's try again."

"Always the harsh taskmaster. Ladies and gentlemen, this may give you a clue as to why I welcomed my wife's retirement from our act," Houdini joked as Mrs. Houdini walked toward a woman and whispered in her ear. The woman willingly handed over her purse, which Bess rummaged through. She returned the purse but kept an object she took from it pressed against her chest.

"I am holding an object I have borrowed. Answer me, Houdini. Say now what it is I hold against my breast."

"Ah, this is difficult. I must think *very* hard. Bess, you must clear your mind of *everything* but the object. Say nothing, just *send* your thoughts to me." During the next few moments of silence, Nate could feel the crowd's growing expectation.

Houdini clapped his hands loudly two times. "You are holding an exquisite face powder case made of . . . made of jade, if I am not mistaken."

"My heavens," exclaimed the woman. "That is a jade piece my husband gave me years ago." Bess opened her hand and exhibited the green powder case for all to see.

"It was made in China, and I have seen only two others like it. How could you possibly have guessed?" the woman asked in amazement.

The audience's hearty applause was punctuated by exclamations of genuine wonderment—an emotion shared by Nate.

"I could not possibly *guess*, madam," Houdini explained. "At the same time, I am not at liberty to explain how I *knew*. Bess, we should not outlast our welcome. Perhaps one more object—a coin. And perhaps Colonel Roosevelt will oblige. He certainly knows that I have not had access to his pockets."

"By George! I don't know what you have had access to, Houdini, but I'm exceedingly doubtful that you could have seen the coin I keep in my vest pocket," Roosevelt excitedly said. "Mrs. Houdini, mentally communicate the mint date of *this* coin, if you possibly can."

"A *challenge* from the former president! Are we up to it, Bess?"

"It will take all of our powers, Houdini. I pray you concentrate before you *try to* tell me the date this coin was minted, please, I urge you to take your time."

"Hmmm. I see the date. Bess, you have sent me the date, but the country of manufacture is not entirely clear."

"I am working on it," his wife said dreamily. "It should become clearer now."

Houdini was silent for what seemed an extraordinarily

long time and then yelled out his answer. "The coin was minted in the Netherlands in the year 1678."

"By thunder! That is correct!" Roosevelt jumped from his chair and stood before the still-blindfolded Houdini. "How could you possibly guess? That coin was given to me a year ago by Queen Wilhelmina of the Netherlands. No one but my wife and children has ever seen it. I am absolutely overwhelmed, Houdini. Blast, how did you do it?"

Houdini deftly untied the blindfold, stood, and bowed to his appreciative audience.

"Overwhelmed enough to cooperate with me?" he asked out of the corner of his smiling mouth.

21

If his performance had been in a theater, Houdini could
easily have waved goodbye and ducked backstage. But
the audience surged forward, forming a circular human
wall around the entertainer and the former president.
Nate saw his mother waving for him and slowly worked
his way across to her.

"Nate, Aunt Alice can't go back in this weather without
a raincoat," she said, pointing to the window. Through the
stained-glass windows Nate could see water sheeting
down. "Will you fetch ours?"

"Of course, Mother. Tell Mrs. Houdini I will send Phin
to her cabin if I can find him."

"He could go to our cabin, too."

"No, I'll go. I need some time to think about a few things." Nate kept wondering if these happy-go-lucky Lynches were conspiring with the elderly man in the soft cap and heavy shoes.

And is he in league with Jumpy?

Near the back of the lounge, Phin and Nate planned to run in opposite directions when they got outside. But Nate couldn't resist putting one over on Phin and broke into a run before reaching the door.

"Eh, that's a cheat!" Phin cried, and broke into a run, too. Nate pushed the exit door so forcefully that it swung open and hit a man, knocking him clean down.

"I'm sorry, sir . . . I never imagined anybody would be standing outside," Nate apologized as he quickly bent to one knee to help the man.

"Blimey, oh blimey," Phin said, rushing to help.

"No harm done. Just leave me alone," the fallen man said.

"But you might be hurt," Nate said.

"I'm perfectly fine," he said, looking into the boy's eyes, his long, thin nose pointing at Nate like a dagger. The splotchy purple wart on his left nostril looked bigger than a baseball.

It's him, it's Jumpy!

Nate fought back an incredible urge to yell out.

Don't let on. Stay calm. I need proof.

"If you don't need any help, I'll just say sorry and get out of the rain," Nate said, trying to keep a steady voice.

"The gentleman needs a 'and," Phin insisted as he helped him stand.

"I'm fine now, really," Jumpy said, looking past Nate and Phin into the crowded lounge. "Too much action in there. I'll go to the smoking room instead."

He walked away unhurriedly and turned onto the main deck.

"That was a close shave. Off we go," Phin said, and attempted to run, but Nate held his coat.

" 'Ere, what are you about?" the bellboy protested.

Nate dragged him to the corner and said: "That's Jumpy!"

"Who's it, then?"

"The gunman—we call him Jumpy."

"Oh, bosh, you're daft as a *bush*," Phin exclaimed.

"Sshh! There's no time to explain. I'm going to follow him. If I find out what cabin he's in, we can search it, find his gun, and arrest him."

"You're bleedin' serious, ain't ya?"

"You fetch the raincoats. I'm going to follow Jumpy," Nate whispered as he took off in pursuit. He heard Phin say something about "barking irons" and "lead," but he didn't stop to listen.

22

Shielding his eyes against the driving rain, Nate clung to the interior alleyway walls and tried to stay a reasonable distance behind his prey. He didn't know what exactly a reasonable distance was—never having followed a man before—but decided he could stay close.

After all, I've got the upper hand. He doesn't know who I am.

Jumpy walked into the grand entrance hall, shook the rain off himself, and casually descended the stair toward B-deck.

He's in no hurry, Nate thought. *Cool as you please.*

On C-deck, Nate's confidence was shaken momentarily when he noticed that Jumpy was not wearing his familiar winter coat. He was in a waterproof mackintosh.

Why not? He probably has plenty of clothing changes to go with the theatrical makeup. Or maybe he's wearing a reversible coat. That's right! In his book Houdini said thieves use reversible coats all the time. Reversible pants, too!

At the D-deck landing, Jumpy left the first-class stairs and walked toward the third-class cabins. They were located on the lower decks and toward the front because the ship's up-and-down movement was most noticeable there. Nate could feel the floor moving under his feet.

The distance between cabin doors was less than in first class, and the alleyways were narrower. Many more people were crammed into less space here than higher up. Through an open door, Nate saw six bunks in a cabin less than half the size of the one he shared with his mother and great-aunt.

Even though this neighborhood of the *Lusitania* reminded him of New York's Lower East Side, the people he passed were all very well dressed and polite.

Near a dining room, Jumpy headed down another stairway—the third-class stairway. It was sturdy and safe, but like everything else in third class, much less grand than its first-class counterpart.

Jumpy left the stairway at F-deck—a deck below the waterline but still crammed with the cabins of paying passengers—and sauntered toward a public lavatory. Nate stayed outside, loitering a few feet away from the door.

Minutes passed and Jumpy didn't reappear. As more time went by, Nate wondered if he had made a mistake.

Maybe the bathroom has a door on the far side. Maybe he left that way. Oh, how could I lose him after all this?

Nobody went in or came out for what seemed like an eternity. Nate couldn't stand just waiting around. He decided to walk in and have a look.

I still have the upper hand, I have to remember that. If he's inside, I'll pretend I need the toilet. But I must see if there's a back door.

Nate strode through the doorway and instantaneously felt an arm encircle his neck from behind. He was turned around and pushed—face-first—against the tiled wall. A cold, circular-shaped piece of metal—the barrel of a gun?—pressed painfully into his right temple.

"Who the devil *are* you, boy?" Jumpy asked, his voice reedy and very angry. Nate could feel Jumpy's heart pounding rapidly against his back.

"Nate Fuller."

"And what the devil does 'Nate Fuller' mean to me? Why are you following me?"

"I'm not following you. You've made a mistake. I just came in to use the bathroom. Let me go and—"

"For God's sake, don't lie to me! You knocked me down outside the lounge and you've been following me ever since. Why?"

Nate wasn't used to lying, but a really good lie now might save his life.

"Well . . . you see—the bellboy and I made a bet. I said that I could shadow somebody for an entire day without—"

"I *know* that you recognized me. When you helped me up, you looked in my eyes and recognized me. Now tell me where from. And no more lies!"

"I remember you from Pier 54. You walked there every day before the ship sailed."

"Where else?"

Nate paused a few seconds, pretending that he was thinking.

"No other place. I remember you from standing on the pier. Now please, let me go."

"You must think I'm an idiot. I remember you! I gave you that lump on the back of your head. Or did you forget?"

"What do you want?" Nate asked, masking his fear with boldness. "Money?"

"I'm going to lower this gun to your side. I'm going to release my arm. You're not going to run or scream or let on in any way that things aren't totally *ipsy-pipsy*. Or else!"

Ipsy-pipsy?

"We're just taking a walk to the front of the deck—together," Jumpy said.

"What then?"

"Just shut up! If you don't, I'll shoot. Understand?"

Nate nodded. Jumpy released his arm grip, lowered the gun, and they left the bathroom just as another passenger walked in.

In a matter of seconds—too short a time even for Nate to hatch an escape plan—they reached the cargo hold. A padlocked steel door faced them. Jumpy told Nate to sit against the wall.

"Pull your knees up. Then hold your hands together under your knees. If you move, I'll shoot."

He tucked the gun under his arm and fished a couple of slender metal pieces out of his inner coat pocket.

"Burglars' tools?" Nate asked without thinking.

"Lock picks, yeah. Don't move. I'll have this door opened in a minute or two." He moved the metal pieces deliberately inside the lock hole, all the time keeping his eye on Nate. They were alone in what had to be the most quiet and least visited area of the ship.

What a position! Nate couldn't possibly get up and run fast enough to get away. What could he do? He knew that Jumpy didn't plan on kidnapping him. It was spur of the moment.

He's making it up as he goes . . . Distract him. That's my only hope.

"Were you going to take another shot at Colonel Roosevelt? Is that why you were outside the lounge?"

"I wasn't there to see that interfering Houdini. I should've killed him. If he hadn't charged me, I would have gotten Roosevelt with the next shot. And I should have shot you. Would have saved me this grief." Jumpy fumbled with the padlock. "Damnation! This is harder than it looks."

Nate mulled over Jumpy's threats and excuses and decided the man was bluffing. Jumpy could have slipped into the lounge and easily walked right up to Roosevelt during the mind-reading exhibition. He couldn't have missed a stationary target, but he couldn't have escaped, either. Clearly, he didn't want to be caught, didn't want to go to prison. He wasn't desperate then.

As Jumpy continued to prod and poke the lock's insides, Nate goaded himself: *Keep talking! Keep distracting him!*

"Why do you want to kill Roosevelt?"

"What do you care?"

"I do care," Nate insisted. "It's not just because he didn't give you a job or something like that, is it?"

"Idiot!" Jumpy stopped fiddling with the burglars' tools and looked Nate squarely in the eye.

"Roosevelt is on a peace mission. He wants to negotiate an end to the arms race between England and Germany. Peace in Europe! That does nobody any good. But a big war—total, global war—that will be good for everybody. In the long run."

"How on earth will it be good?" Nate asked with genuine curiosity.

"Because the war will impoverish them. The gun makers and shipbuilders, they'll profit at first, but they'll get squeezed eventually." Jumpy was becoming increasingly passionate. "If enough innocent men die in a senseless war, people will revolt. All the kings and archdukes and tsars—and even presidents—will fall. There'll be total anarchy. When all the slates are wiped clean, then common men and women will have their say. The weak and downtrodden will rise up."

"And killing Roosevelt will help bring down the kings?"

"It will help create chaos. And chaos will bring about justice. In the long run."

Jumpy looked back toward the padlocked door and redoubled his efforts.

Nate could not think of anything to say about the man's political ideas except that they sounded crazy, so he said the first thing that popped into his head: "Are you going to lock me in the baggage compartment?"

Jumpy didn't answer.

"You're going to bind and gag me, I guess. So they won't find me until you escape from the ship in Liverpool?"

"*I'm* not an idiot, boy. They start moving the trunks before docking. I'm going to bury you alive in a steamer trunk. You'll be dead by tomorrow."

Jumpy turned, pulled the gun from under his armpit, and aimed it to make his point. "None of *this* would have been necessary if you had minded your own business and played shuffleboard or deck tennis instead of snooping."

"But what if I promise not to say anything? Really, I will give you a solemn oath," Nate pleaded, knowing he was bargaining for his life.

Jumpy shook his head and said, "Too late, kid. No good!"

"I'll say *no good*, you bleedin' coward!"

It was Phin.

23

Jumpy practically jumped out of his skin at the sound of Phin's voice. Dropping the lock picks, he aimed the gun down the corridor, toward the voice.

The wall Nate leaned against was at the end of a passage about ten feet wide that branched into two alleyways leading back toward passenger compartments. Phin was hidden in one or the other.

"Who are you?" Jumpy demanded. "Show yourself."

"I'm an officer on this ship, and you're caught bang to rights, you are. Drop that iron an' surrender."

"You're a boy. You shouldn't play games like this," Jumpy warned. "Come help me with your friend. He's been hurt."

"A right brassy bastard you are," Phin shot back. "I 'eard everything."

"Come out now or I'll shoot your friend," Jumpy threatened, turning the pistol back on Nate.

"Don't!" Nate warned.

"Come here!"

"So you can drill us both? Not a chance," Phin said.

"Your friend has five seconds to live. Four! Three!"

"I don't think that's true," Nate said, scrambling to his feet.

"One more step and I'll shoot!"

"You will not," Nate retorted, trying to sound confident as he edged away, the gun's muzzle following him.

" 'E's all mouth and no trousers!" Phin yelled.

"No! He's no coward. But he's not here to kill us," Nate said as he inched toward freedom. "If he shoots me, that's the end of it. You'll get away and he'll be caught. He'll be a total failure, because shooting me won't cause a war between England and Germany."

"A war?" Phin yelled. "What blinkin' war?"

"He *must* kill Roosevelt," Nate continued. He looked directly into Jumpy's eyes as he spoke, pretending the indecisive assassin had no gun trained on him.

"The only way he can do that," Nate said, taking a deep breath and turning his back toward Jumpy, "the only way is to let us walk away."

Nate took two slow, deliberate steps. He caught sight of Phin plastered to the wall in the alleyway to the left.

Stretching his eyebrows upward and mouthing *Go!* Nate silently urged Phin to run. The bellboy understood and took off. Nate broke into a run and was on his heels in a flash.

They dashed around walls and up stairs until a steward grabbed Phin and lectured him about unprofessional behavior. Nate caught his breath and checked to see if they were being pursued before coming to his rescuer's rescue.

24

Nate was torn about what to do next.

Should he go to his stateroom and let his mother know he was all right? That would mean telling her and Aunt Alice what had happened since he'd left the lounge to fetch rain gear.

Should he find Colonel Roosevelt and tell him that Jumpy was on the prowl? But he had no idea where Roosevelt was.

The best idea was telling Houdini and getting his advice. As he and Phin walked toward the Houdinis' suite, Nate's fright diminished. It was replaced by an overwhelming desire to tell their epic tale of courage in the face of certain death.

"Phin, I will do the talking," he said, getting the sequence of events straight in his mind.

"But I was there, in the thick of it," protested the bellboy.

"I'm glad you were, but, well, Houdini will understand me more easily."

"Understand, is it? Bilge!"

"Why were you there?" asked Nate.

"I never miss a party," Phin said with a broad grin. "I told another bellboy to get the coats and 'Oodini would drop 'im 'alf a crown straightaway. Then I doubled back on you."

"I'm glad you did, that's for sure," Nate said as he knocked on the suite door.

It swung open to give him more of a shock than a surprise.

"So it's you, lad," said the elderly man who had been following Nate since dawn. He wasn't wearing his soft-brimmed cap, but it was unquestionably the same man. "Good thing we didn't raise the hue and cry to find you. This is no weather to be out and about."

Nate was at a complete loss.

They've got Houdini. And now me!

"Is that my Nate?" The cabin door opened wide, and Deborah Fuller brushed past the elderly man to embrace her son. "I've been so worried. Where have you been?"

"Tell us all," Houdini said weakly from inside. "But be

so kind as to come in and close the door. Keep the typhoon outside."

"No comedy, Houdini!" Mrs. Houdini said. "Do not pretend that you were unconcerned."

Nate floated into the room feeling dazed and confused. He couldn't take his eyes off the man who had opened the door.

Houdini's penetrating mind seemed to read Nate's thoughts instantly. "Tatum, please introduce yourself to my young friend."

"Arthur Tatum, Metropolitan Police Inspector, retired. Currently undercover operative aboard the *Lusitania*." He shook Nate's hand furiously.

"Metropolitan Police? You mean Scotland Yard," Nate said.

"One and the same," Tatum replied cheerily.

"I tol' you 'e was a rozzer," Phin said.

"Why were you shadowing me?" Nate asked.

"You are a bright lad. Well-trained," Tatum added, tipping an imaginary cap in the direction of Houdini. For the first time, Nate noticed that Houdini was lying on a sofa with a blanket draped over him.

"Self-taught," Houdini said weakly. The storm—fierce enough now to rock even this huge a ship—must have brought on a bout of seasickness. The constant rise and fall of the ship had made Nate feel queasy, but he didn't think that qualified as real seasickness.

"As may be," Tatum replied. "I was not tailing you, young sir, and I regret any inconvenience I may have caused. My orders from London were to make myself available to Mr. Houdini without revealing my identity to anyone else. Unfortunately, he was always with you or your former president or the captain. A very popular man you are, Mr. Houdini."

"I suppose that I am. And just Houdini will do."

"So it was only a coincidence that you spoke with the Lynches on deck this morning—and they volunteered for the mind-reading session and that they have been near Colonel Roosevelt all day?" Nate asked.

"Entirely coincidental, I would say," Tatum replied.

"I agree, but good thinking," Houdini said. "I sent a wireless to Captain Root inquiring about them, just in case." Houdini lifted a weighty book that had been leaning against the sofa. Nate could see the word *Ledger* embossed on its cover. Opening the book with it propped on his lap, Houdini flipped the pages until he found the one he wanted and began writing.

A ledger? Is Houdini doing bookkeeping now?

"As may be. Now the cat's out of the bag right and proper about me," Tatum said regretfully. "With Mrs. Houdini and Mrs. Fuller, and now you and this bellboy knowing who I am, I don't suppose there is any chance of me doing my real job on this voyage."

"What job was that?" Mrs. Houdini asked.

"Catching card cheats, madam. A trio of them—and

very slick they are—has been working the North Atlantic for months. Last month they netted a cool five thousand from some first-class gentleman passengers on the *Queen Victoria*. One of their twists—er, pardon me, ladies—one of their female acquaintances was arrested and told the Yard that these sharks would be on *this* passage of the *Lusitania*."

"You're an expert on card cheating, Inspector Tatum?" Nate asked.

"Just Tatum is sufficient, young sir," the inspector jested.

"Just Nate for me!"

Tatum erupted in such lusty laughter that everyone joined in.

"Laughter lightens your load," he said finally. "Yes, after twenty years as a fraud and vice detective, I am London's expert on card manipulation."

"*Dishonest* card manipulation," corrected Mrs. Houdini, prompting another round of laughs.

"Nate, you appear well," Houdini said. "Have you been doing anything of interest for the last hour or so?"

Nate realized that the exciting but concise tale he had prepared before entering the suite had simply evaporated from his mind. Phin looked at his tongue-tied friend and rolled his eyes. But after hemming and hawing a moment, Nate just plunged in. "Well, here's what happened . . ."

25

By the time Nate was finished, he was convinced the retelling had taken twice as long as the events themselves. And not because he had invented or exaggerated anything. It was the interruptions. His audience constantly asked him to restate what he had just said. They even stopped him to guess at what happened next rather than letting him simply say what happened next.

They interrupted so often Nate felt that he must be a terrible reporter—to be so unclear. Only Houdini listened without comment, still scribbling occasionally in his ledger.

Maybe he is just totally bored, Nate told himself.

"Phenomenal report," Houdini exclaimed. "Someday you could be a first-rate war correspondent, Nate. Already you are a one hundred percent hero."

Nate felt his face flush at the compliment and at the gushing attention his mother and Mrs. Houdini lavished on him.

"Let us not forget young Newborn's courage," said Houdini.

"It wasn't anything," Phin replied with a bow.

"Indeed it was!" Houdini insisted. "You both risked your safety for another's."

"And that must not happen again," Deborah Fuller said. "I cannot allow it to happen again."

"I was never really in danger, Mother."

"I will not listen to that sort of . . . misrepresentation, *Nathaniel*."

"What has happened is intolerable, Deborah," Houdini said in a calming voice. "Nate has been in terrible danger. Several times in only two days. It is appalling! But it happened only because you have raised a bright, observant, courageous son. I'm sure you do not regret that."

"Of course I don't regret that, Houdini. I am incredibly proud of Nate. And I want to be just as proud when I am as old as his great-aunt."

"Well said, my dear lady. None of us should ever be in Jumpy's gunsights again. I have a plan."

Houdini carefully ripped a page from his ledger and

passed it to Phin. "Take that to the editor of the ship's newspaper. Make certain he gets it personally and knows that it comes from me."

"Right, guv. Ina flash." The bellboy darted out of the cabin.

"A plan—that's a relief," Tatum said unexpectedly. Seeing a few curious looks thrown in his direction, he explained: "I never ran across a political assassin before. More comfortable with forgers and confidence men."

The plan of action that Houdini outlined pleased all present, except for Nate. "I don't understand. You mean we're going to let him walk off the ship?"

"Hopefully, into the arms of dozens of Scotland Yard men," Houdini answered.

"But we could set a trap."

"Could we? With Colonel Roosevelt or you as the cheese?"

"Nathaniel Greene Makeworthy Fuller, enough is enough!" Deborah Fuller said with a long pause after each word.

"Listen to your elders, young man," counseled Tatum. "This Jumpy fellow is like a wounded lion or tiger—too dangerous to track. Best throw a net over him in Liverpool."

Nate saw Mrs. Houdini nod in agreement and knew the vote was four-to-one against. He decided to make one last try, anyway.

"But isn't it our duty—"

"You're too young to talk about duty," Nate's mother said angrily.

"If I may, Deborah," Houdini said gently. "One is never too young to understand duty. I've often said it's only right that whatever brains and gifts *I* have should benefit humanity in some greater way than merely entertaining people. But no one benefits if I stand in front of a moving train. Or a loaded gun."

"I understand *that*," Nate said. "Still—"

"Still nothing, Nate. None of us here is an active-duty policeman. If—when—this ship docks without anyone else being shot, we will have played our part." Houdini said it with such finality that Nate knew the discussion had ended.

"Tatum, would you ask Colonel Roosevelt to join us— offering apologies that I am too ill-disposed to join him?"

"What should Nate and I do?" asked Nate's mother.

"Difficult to say," Houdini answered truthfully. "It is almost impossible that Jumpy could recognize you as Nate's mother. Even if he can, we have no idea whether he wants to tangle with Nate again."

Nate enjoyed the unexpected idea that a wanted criminal might be afraid to tangle with him.

"But he is resourceful. He may be able to find your cabin. Nate did volunteer his name."

Ouch! That was a slip, telling him my real name.

"I'm sure that Aunt Alice is frantic," Deborah said.

"Houdini, this suite has a telephone," Mrs. Houdini exclaimed.

"A telephone? What unbelievable luxury. Who can we call?" The *Lusitania* was the first steamship with telephone service for passengers, but only passengers in the most expensive staterooms.

"We can call the captain and ask him to send several men in uniform to escort Deborah and Nate to their stateroom."

"Let it be done!" Houdini said with a wave of the arm. "With one caveat. Deborah, allow Nate to remain here."

"Oh, yes!" Nate said, thinking that it would be much better if his mother explained everything to Aunt Alice alone. "I can help here."

"Can he really be helpful?" Nate's mother asked.

"Unquestionably. The colonel can be very stubborn. We need all the troops we can muster."

"My darling husband," Mrs. Houdini said, pressing a cold compress against his forehead. "Give him a madman on the loose and his seasickness practically cures itself. Deborah, would you like moral support when you speak with Aunt Alice?"

26

The impromptu melodrama Houdini had staged for Colonel Roosevelt—aided by natural storm sounds—worked like a charm. Roosevelt's resistance melted instantly. He agreed to any and all protective measures Houdini recommended, after it was made clear that his pride might get poor, innocent young Nate killed—as well as Nate's family and the Houdinis and anyone else who got in the way.

Nate regretted that his role was restricted to sitting quietly on the floor, legs crossed, near Houdini. He was a prop, not a character. He was tempted at one point to ask whether Jumpy had enough ammunition to carry out all of the mayhem Houdini predicted—just to see how his mentor would react. But he wisely resisted that temptation.

"The inconvenience will really be minor, Colonel," Houdini said to soften the blow.

"It will not be *minor*, but I will not be reckless with the lives of others," Roosevelt said. "I would happily abide with the fall of the dice; I cannot expect that of Nate or you."

"Considering the weather, you are not giving up that much," Houdini said. Wind still howled outside; rain lashed against the exterior metal walls of the suite's sitting room.

"The captain suggested that you take his first officer's cabin on the bridge deck. There is a bath attached, and the officers' smoking room next door will be your office until we reach Liverpool. A typewriter operator will be available. The captain's chef and private dining room will be at your disposal."

"I hope he doesn't expect me to take meals with him. That ocean liner sailor is so exceedingly arrogant . . . he positively makes my blood boil," Roosevelt said, the color in his face rising.

"The bridge deck will be locked and closed to visitors. The officer on duty will have a gun at hand," Houdini calmly continued.

"Of course, I will have my Colt also," Roosevelt said, tapping his side.

"I'm glad you reminded me about that gun, Colonel.

Tatum has no weapon and could use one to protect Nate and his family. Would you lend it to him?"

Roosevelt stiffened to resist, then rose and removed his suit coat. "A deal is a deal, after all. I agreed that you make the rules." He unhooked the latch that held his leather holster in place and extended the sheathed pistol in his hands. "You should know that this revolver has sentimental value. I carried it throughout the Cuban campaign," he said.

"Duly noted," Houdini said.

Roosevelt thrust the weapon into Nate's hands. It was far heavier than Nate expected.

"Never handled a gun before, Nate?" the former president asked.

"I have not, Colonel. It's no wonder that Jumpy knocked me out when he hit me with his."

"My final request, Colonel," said Houdini. "You cannot walk on the promenade for exercise. That would be inviting another attempt."

"Blast this infernal anarchist. I will continue to use the exercise machinery in the gym."

"Colonel, you cannot. It is too public; console yourself by exercising your mind."

"That smoking room is very large," Nate said out of the blue.

Houdini and Roosevelt both acknowledged that fact.

"Well, since the captain is moving things around, why not remove the table and replace it with a writing desk and chairs? That would leave room for exercise machines."

"Brilliant lad. Absolutely cunning," Roosevelt declared. "I will tell the captain when I see him."

"Why wait? Please call from the phone in the next room," Houdini said.

The former president did just that, leaving Nate and Houdini alone.

"All has gone according to plan, Nate. Better than planned, because of you. Please put that gun behind the table, out of sight until Tatum returns."

Nate obliged, hiding the weapon.

"You will be able to move about under Tatum's protection. Tell me if I am wrong, but I do not think Jumpy will risk his life to revenge himself upon you."

"I do agree. Entirely," Nate said confidently. "If he has the nerve to attack again, he will attack the colonel. I can't see my death causing chaos in Europe."

"Nor mine; he has no interest in me."

"I don't agree with that," Nate said. "He blames you for his failure. He seemed pretty angry with you. And he *said* he should have killed you, *too*! You need protection."

"There is only one Tatum, Nate. He cannot be in two places at once."

"He wouldn't need to be if . . ."

"If what?"

Nate was careful not to sound too eager as he explained. Since his mother, great-aunt, and Mrs. Houdini were not targets, they were not in harm's way. If Mrs. Houdini took Nate's bed, the ladies—who enjoyed one another's company anyway—would be safer. That way, Houdini could recuperate in his bedroom. Nate and Tatum could sleep comfortably in the sitting room.

"And if, just if, Jumpy goes looking for you?"

"I expect that junior ship's officers would stand guard at night. Maybe walk with the ladies during the day—if the weather ever improves. And I thought—for total security—Mrs. Houdini could use your trick at night."

"My trick?" Houdini asked.

"Yes, the antiburglar trick you described in *The Right Way to Do Wrong.*"

"Bless my soul, yes. A wooden wedge in the door, secured by a screw in the floor. When the colonel finishes with the phone, call the Enquiry Desk and see if they can send us a carpenter. Then we need Phin or another bellboy. I must make a few edits in tomorrow's newspaper story. It will read better after I've added your ideas."

"I say, Houdini, you will not use this security panic or your seasickness to wriggle out of your promise," Roosevelt said, returning to the sitting room.

"You mean an illusion to leave you speechless?"

"Will you honor that promise?"

"I think of nothing else," Houdini said with a sincerity that astonished Nate.

27

After two physically and mentally exhausting days at sea, Nate was content to watch others at work. First the bellboys carried several bags of Mrs. Houdini's essentials to Nate's cabin. Later they returned with a satchel of the boy's clothing and toiletries, which for the time being remained by the door, unopened. One bellboy, snickering at the inert landlubbers, joked, "The weather must be rough on you, sirs. We crew don't even notice when *Lucy* puts her foot in a hole now and then."

Nate roused himself to help Tatum devour a tray of sandwiches delivered from the kitchen, but begged off walking Charlie. The terrier dragged only Phin into the storm, a result that obviously pleased the retired detective.

"Better that the dog goes out on a night like this and the man stays dry."

"But Phin went with him," Nate said.

"That is what he is paid for, lad," Tatum answered.

Watching the comings and goings, Houdini said, "I shudder to think of the tips I will owe the staff when we arrive."

When Nate finally unpacked, he discovered two letters, which he saved for bedtime. The first was from his mother:

> Nate, my precious, you certainly are seeing more of Houdini on this voyage than I anticipated! I am sure you are making the most of it.
>
> I love you dearly, and you know I would simply *die* if you were harmed. When you read this, please make one silent promise to me—that you will not do anything or go anywhere without consulting with Houdini and Inspector Tatum beforehand. Do that now, please.

Nate paused and thought. He couldn't bring himself to make a promise that he knew he might break.

> Do not worry about us. We *ladies* will have a splendid time. Bess is good company for me and has a gracious manner with Aunt Alice that I envy. We will enjoy ourselves. Enjoy yourself—snug in that suite.

The second letter was from Aunt Alice.

Nathaniel, I fully expect you to behave appropriately. Difficult circumstances are the ultimate test of a superior character. I am confident that you will pass that test as your father and my husband, Arthur, did before you.

Remember that your unusual living arrangement is no excuse for misbehavior.

Attend to your personal hygiene as you would at home.

Do not lapse into the misconduct typically exhibited by policemen and burlesque performers because you are required to associate with them. (I must admit that the dignified and respectable behavior displayed by Mrs. Houdini gives me hope for her husband.)

Be on guard!

Hardly aware that he had dropped the letters, the exhausted Nate burrowed into the blankets on the sofa. Seeing Tatum engrossed in solitaire—Roosevelt's Colt revolver at the ready—and hearing Houdini moan occasionally from the next room, he drifted into well-earned sleep.

28

A volley of rapid gunfire woke Nate a second later. He rolled from the sofa in terror and crawled for cover behind it. Another volley of three shots was fired. Except this time, Nate wasn't certain they were shots.

"It's just a bad dream, lad."

Nate thought he recognized the voice coming from above. He rolled onto his back and saw Tatum.

"Just a bad dream. Not unusual, considering. I better answer that knocking before he gets impatient and kicks the door in."

"I thought . . . I thought it was . . . something else," Nate said, scrambling to his feet and scrambling for words at the same time.

Three more raps on the door—louder than before.

"Hold your horses!" Tatum yelled. He turned toward Nate and said, "I know what you thought. Nothing unusual at all."

"If you say so."

"I do," he said, and opened the door. Phin and Charlie practically tumbled in.

"I got the mornin' rag, and it's 'ot. All 'Oodini and Roosevelt and 'the gunman,' " the bellboy cried.

"It's morning already?" Nate couldn't believe it.

"Still knackered, 'e is," Phin joked as he bent over to release Charlie from his leash. Tatum snatched the newspapers from his hand and passed one to Nate.

"Read it for us, would you?" the inspector suggested.

Nate started with the headlines.

DAYLIGHT MURDER ATTEMPTED

GUNMAN FOILED BY QUICK-WITTED PASSENGER

ARREST EXPECTED SOON

" 'Ere now, 'ow you goin' to clap ruffles on 'im when you can't lay 'ands on 'im?" Phin broke in.

"We will certainly handcuff him in Liverpool, where we will be soon enough," Tatum said.

Nate read the story itself:

148

The gunman responsible for the unsuccessful attempt on the life of Theodore Roosevelt, former president of the United States, and the serious injury of Roosevelt's traveling companion, Thomas Flanagan, struck again yesterday.

The villain abducted a witness to the original shooting with the intention of killing said witness. The kidnapping victim—whose name is being withheld—managed to trick his captor and escape unharmed. (Well done!)

Inspector Arthur Tatum of New Scotland Yard, a passenger, has assumed responsibility for the safety of Mr. Roosevelt and the unnamed witness / kidnapping victim.

The inspector informed this reporter that "a significant number of passengers and crew members witnessed yesterday's crime. They are ready to identify the criminal in an identity parade when he is apprehended." He added that "certain facts which cannot be released at this time *guarantee*" that the gunman will be apprehended shortly.

Inspector Tatum is so confident of making an arrest before docking that he has given approval for the great Houdini's planned mystical extravaganza. "Houdini promised Colonel Roosevelt some sort of demonstration during the fancy-dress party," Tatum told us, "and I see no reason to disappoint people. By the time of that party, the coast will be clear. We will have the gunman in irons, rest assured."

When asked for details of his upcoming performance, Mr. Houdini told this reporter, "I have something unique, something astonishing, planned to entertain the former president. Come to the first-class lounge prepared to be amazed."

Readers will be pleased to note that the life of Mr. Flanagan, Mr. Roosevelt's traveling companion, was saved through the skilled intervention of Sir Roland Hanna, member of the Royal College of Surgeons. Mr. Flanagan is expected to make a full recovery.

"Makes me sound a sight more confident than I am," Tatum commented.

"As Shakespeare said, we all have our parts to play," Houdini said, using the bedroom doorframe to support himself. He walked into the room slowly, relying on his cane for balance.

"And Inspector Tatum's part is scaring Jumpy, right?" Nate asked. "Frightening Jumpy so much that he stays in hiding?"

"As may be," Tatum said. "I would like it better if we could nobble the devil."

"Who wouldn't? But the stakes are too high to tempt fate," Houdini said as he glanced at Nate, while Tatum nodded his agreement.

"What if someone actually did see Jumpy, recognized him from one of the dining rooms or going in and out of his cabin?" Nate asked.

"The more I consider our quandary, the more I doubt that possibility."

"Because he has help?" Nate asked.

"A handler, more likely. His lack of resolve—his timidity—makes me think of him as a poorly trained attack dog. He lacks what some call a 'killer instinct.' I think his master keeps him kenneled until he sends him out to kill."

"The Lynches could be his handlers."

"As could a hundred, nay, a thousand other passengers," Tatum said.

"Anything is possible," Houdini admitted. "We'll hear from Captain Root in New York eventually."

"This may be that," Tatum said as he pulled an envelope from his jacket. "Arrived for you while everyone was sleeping."

Houdini sat and read the wireless message.

"Hmm, Root says they check out. Jackie Lynch worked for the city, announced that he had inherited property in Ireland, quit his job, booked passage on the *Lusitania*, and hasn't been seen since. No arrest records. One curious thing: the landlord found 'some personal items' under the bed which they forgot to pack. A pity they are not described in the Marconigram. Still, we lack grounds to think they are involved."

"You cannot search a man's home, or his stateroom, because he is forgetful," Tatum said.

Nate was disappointed but quickly thought of an explanation. "Just because they're rich, that doesn't mean they *couldn't* be anarchists, does it?"

"Heaven help us," Tatum exclaimed. "That's just what the Yard needs—country squires toting guns and carrying bombs."

"Anything is possible," Houdini repeated. "*Such* is life."

"I'll say. I did as much as 'e did to foil the bludger. An' I don't get any ink," Phin said dejectedly.

"It's criminal," Nate said. Phin obviously did not realize that publishing his name would put him in as much danger as Nate was in.

29

According to Phin, Nate spent that entire day pottering. Nate was reluctant to give Phin the upper hand and brushed the comment aside until the bellboy left on one of his repeated errands for Houdini.

"Tatum, what is pottering?" Nate asked.

Lifting his head from a solitaire layout, the inspector made a show of thinking before he said: "I believe pottering is the aimless pursuit of a trivial activity. Much like playing this game."

"Darn, we *are* wasting our time," Nate said, slamming down a book he had borrowed from Houdini's portable library. "I mean, Houdini is seasick and probably won't recover until the weather improves, but there's nothing wrong with us."

"I am content with that."

"But wouldn't you like to walk down the gangplank with Jumpy in handcuffs? We have two more days to find him."

"If wishes were horses, my father used to say."

"We should do *something*," Nate insisted.

The retired detective gave him a long, sympathetic look. He swept the cards into a pile and gestured for the boy to sit across from him.

"What are we going to do?"

"Play gin rummy. I am happy to teach you if you have never played."

Nate hadn't, but the rules were simple and he found the game diverting. And sitting opposite Tatum gave him the opportunity to interrogate a detective.

It surprised Nate to learn that the biggest case Tatum had ever cracked—in thirty years with the London Metropolitan Police—was that of an expert check forger. Nate realized that he had started at the top of the field, catching a multiple murderer on his first case.

And Nate thought the gentle gray-haired man was kidding him about this being the first time he had ever carried a gun.

"They are dangerous things. People get hurt. It is a gentleman's agreement, you might say, that English criminals do not carry guns, so English police do not need them either," Tatum explained.

Nate finally got around to the question that really fascinated him. "When you were shadowing Houdini—and I thought you were following me—I couldn't positively tell whether you were following me or not. But I didn't fool Jumpy at all. What do you do to fool people, so they don't know they're being followed?"

"Well, I don't know how American detectives do it. We follow four rules," Tatum said. "First, stay behind your subject if you possibly can. Second, never try to hide—"

"That's right. You never tried to hide from me," Nate commented.

"I did not, because you cannot. Where was I, then? . . . Yes, third, act natural no matter what happens. And—"

"You acted natural when I walked toward you. You acted like you were looking for a lost coin."

"Did I indeed? I don't remember. It's second nature, I suppose."

"What is the fourth rule?"

"The fourth rule is probably the most important: Never look your subject eye to eye. The dance is over when you make eye contact," Tatum said, shaking his head.

Nate committed the advice to memory.

Between gin rummy and detective talk, he and Tatum pottered together for hours. After they tired of card playing, Nate split his time between entertaining Charlie and staring at the pages of his book, unable to concentrate.

Try as he might, Nate could not reconcile his mind to the *plan*. He studied the recent entries in his red leather journal. Over the last two days he had logged careful entries about Roosevelt and Houdini being shot, and about being pistol-whipped by Jumpy, recognizing and following Jumpy, then being abducted at gunpoint and walking away unscathed. Nate feared that his last entry would be "English police arrest Jumpy while I stand by." *A loafer, idly watching.*

Nate tossed and turned that night, restless with the recognition of his powerlessness. He was happy when a dry dawn cracked through the curtains—the storm was over at last. And happier still when a call from the bridge invited him to take some exercise and breakfast with Colonel Roosevelt—a surefire cure for boredom.

Nate scanned every face as he and Tatum walked to the bridge deck. Dozens of passengers were on the decks, but Jumpy wasn't among them. Nate glanced over his shoulder at the bridge door, disappointed not to spot his archenemy.

Tatum stayed on the navigating bridge to drink tea and swap stories with the crew while Nate headed into the makeshift domain of Colonel Roosevelt, who had greatly altered the officers' smoking room to fit his tastes. A bookcase stood against one wall. A plush reading chair and floor lamp were positioned nearby. Against another wall was a writing desk strewn with papers. Most of the room was now taken up by a stationary bicycle and a rowing machine. The colonel, dressed in knee-length linen knickerbockers, canvas tennis shoes, and an undershirt, was rowing furiously.

"You're here! Bully! Change in the bathroom there," Roosevelt said without missing a stroke. Nate owned no athletic clothes beyond his school gym outfit. And he had not packed that for his European trip. He decided to strip to his underwear and hope that the colonel wouldn't be offended. When he returned in undershirt, shorts, and brown leather shoes, and climbed upon the bicycle, the colonel noticed—bad eyesight or not.

"No exercise clothes"—huff, huff—"no regular exercise regimen"—huff, huff—"am I right?" the colonel asked while stroking furiously.

"No, not when I'm out of school," Nate said sheepishly. "I get plenty there," he said, pedaling faster and faster to prove his point.

"You need exercise every day. Tennis, boxing, hiking, swimming—they will make you stronger"—huff, huff—"and you will learn to love them."

Roosevelt stopped abruptly and mopped his face with a towel.

"When I was a lad your age, I was sickly. Puny. I *made* my body! You must *make* yours!"

Nate didn't know what to say. He didn't enjoy most of the games he played in gym. He hiked and swam with kids in Connecticut during the summer, but you couldn't hike or swim in Manhattan.

"My boy, I did not invite you here for a lecture, did I? Let's see you work up a sweat for a while."

They exercised for at least a quarter of an hour before Roosevelt said he would bathe, allowing Nate to use the rowing machine. By the time he had finished, Nate had worked up a sweat and needed a bath, too. That turned out to be an unusually pleasant experience.

At home, there was enough hot water in the sink faucets to wash up, but a bath meant you had to heat water in a tank that sat above the tub. Seeing no tank, Nate ran the bathtub faucet and was amazed that the tub filled with hot water—and only minutes after Roosevelt had used it. Nate decided that all the heat from the coal fires powering the ship must be channeled into heating bathwater.

A good thing we don't have this in New York, he thought as he scrubbed himself. *Aunt Alice would have us all bathing every day.*

As they breakfasted privately in the officers' mess, Roosevelt asked an unexpected question. "Nate, I am completely mystified by your great-aunt's hostility toward me. I cannot recall ever knowing an Alice Ludlow from New York City. Can you enlighten me?"

"Well, the thing is, Aunt Alice didn't have any children

of her own. And so my father was like a son to her—she's always said that."

"And did I ever meet your father?" Roosevelt asked.

"I believe you did, sir, though I can't say for sure. My father was a Rough Rider."

"A Rough Rider . . . named Fuller?"

"He was Corporal Nathaniel Greene Makeworthy Fuller the Third," Nate said proudly.

"Corporal Fuller? By Gad, yes! Corporal Fuller. He was your father," Roosevelt said, distracted by his thoughts.

He concentrated on Nate, squinting through his thick spectacles. "You're barely old enough to be a Rough Rider's son."

"I was born after my father's death. He didn't know my mother was expecting when he volunteered."

"And then he died from fever, didn't he?"

"He did," Nate said.

Roosevelt and Nate looked at each other silently for a moment.

"Can you tell me about him?" Nate asked.

"I'm exceedingly pleased to. Your father was a first-class soldier. He was a born leader. Promoted almost immediately to corporal, I recall."

The former president spent the rest of their meal regaling Nate with stories about his father and the liberation of Cuba. He seemed to recall every chance meeting he'd had with Corporal Fuller. For nearly an hour, Roosevelt fleshed out a vivid picture of the father Nate never met. A brave, honest, likable man, respected by his colleagues and his commander.

Nate used all his powers of concentration. He was determined to remember everything so he could share it later with his mother and Aunt Alice.

The spell was broken by Tatum, who peeked his head in to ask when Nate would be ready to leave.

"It is time for other business," Roosevelt said. "I must give you some advice that I have given my own sons, Nate. You were incredibly *brave* when you attempted to stop the man who wounded Flanagan and Houdini. But you were *not* wise. Remember this: *Optimism* is a good characteristic. But if carried to an excess, it becomes *foolishness*. Do not hit a man unless you can put him *to sleep*."

"I'll remember that, and everything that we've talked about," Nate said as he shook the colonel's hand.

"Bully!"

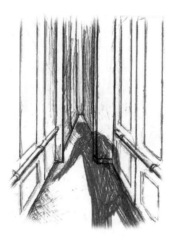

30

An officer coming on duty buttonholed Tatum as he and Nate were leaving the bridge. He had a tip about the cardsharps.

"I should hear this," Tatum said.

"I'll wait outside then. I'd like some sun and fresh air."

"As may be. Collect them near this door, please."

But Nate couldn't resist taking the narrow ladder stairs down to the A-deck promenade to observe people more closely. There were still five "maybes" unaccounted for in his journal. Jumpy was the only "maybe" he'd seen so far.

Fat chance of finding the others with a bodyguard every minute.

The sun was blotted out over his right shoulder. Glancing upward, Nate saw the wide, flat brim of a man's black hat. Under the brim an exceedingly tall, thin man with a sharp, hawklike nose hovered above him. Nate then noticed the white collar and black shirt that distinguished him as a man of the cloth.

"Can I be of help, Reverend?"

"You can, my son. You can carry an urgent message to President Roosevelt. I've seen you in his company. You might be so kind as to introduce me to the president," the minister said, smiling.

"I couldn't do that, sir, without knowing who you are. And what your business is with the colonel." Nate swelled with a sense of official power.

"I am the Reverend Jeremiah Ludd, minister to the faithful in the village of Gotham in the county of Notts, England."

"I am—" Nate stopped abruptly, not ready to make the same mistake twice—giving his name to a stranger. "I am a friend of Colonel Roosevelt's. What is your urgent message, Reverend?"

"Plainly speaking, the Great Designer made the mighty Atlantic Ocean as a terrible, awe-inspiring *barrier* between continents. But today, because of ships like this and their scientific *technology*, we speak of the ocean casually, as nothing greater than a *herring pond*. They build vessels to act like river ferries, denying the ocean's power . . ."

The Reverend Ludd's voice rose and fell in oratorical

style. His passion was meant to rivet one's attention, but it quickly had the opposite effect on Nate. It lulled him into a thoughtful reverie, the way all sermons did.

Nate recalled the story of "The Bishop" from Houdini's book about criminals. The Bishop was a confidence man from Missouri who—dressed as an Episcopalian bishop—bilked a fortune from London store owners. And he got away with it because none of the store owners were bold enough to accuse a clergyman of criminal activity.

Nate's only reason for questioning Reverend Ludd was the man's eagerness to meet Roosevelt. But he made the logical leap that no person could be a better handler or protector for Jumpy than a minister.

"Don't you see?" Ludd thundered, grabbing Nate by his shoulders and shaking him. "We are flying in the face of Nature. We are asking for the Almighty's wrath."

Realizing he hadn't been listening at all, Nate asked a vague, general question to get back into the flow. "How can we avoid that, Reverend?"

"By scuttling this ship and all ships like it," Ludd said triumphantly, as if very pleased with himself.

"Scuttling? Do you mean purposely sinking this ship?"

"Not with passengers aboard," Ludd said. "But this is no mere ship. It is an *insult* to the Almighty. A vileness created by atheistic scientists. Intended to *abolish the very fear of God* that is vital for the salvation of poor, simple folk like my parishioners."

Nate's thoughts turned from the idea that the Reverend was a criminal mastermind in disguise to the possibility that he was a genuine lunatic.

"I'll wager they are more simple than poor, Reverend," said a man walking toward Nate and the minister.

It was Jackie Lynch.

"Might you explain your meaning, sir?" Ludd asked in a guarded tone.

"It seems they are simple enough to pay your first-class passage, so they cannot be too poor," Lynch said with a broad smile.

"That's true, Reverend," Nate chimed in. "I understand from my aunt Alice that the fare is quite steep."

"You mock the word of God?" Ludd said.

"I don't recall anything along the lines of 'Thou shalt scuttle the *Lusitania*' in my Bible," Lynch said with a smile. "Although it does say quite a bit about the meek and downtrodden masses you claim to represent."

Nate was impressed. He had never imagined anyone arguing with a minister this way. Let alone getting the best of the argument.

"Are you an atheist?" Ludd asked angrily.

Lynch ignored the question and turned toward Nate. "I remember an outraged sermon I read a few years ago," he said. "A minister called the Boston subway system 'an infernal un-Christian monster sponsored by the *Devil* himself.' He wanted the holes filled and forgotten."

"What a *bad* idea," Nate said. "I take the New York subway all the time."

"And probably never met the Devil there, did you?" Lynch asked.

"And what is it they say?" asked the late-arriving Tatum. "The devil you do know is better than the devil you don't! Pardon us, Reverend, sir, but the lad and I have an appointment. Must leave immediately."

Tatum put a hand in the small of Nate's back and pushed him forward. When they were clear of Ludd and Lynch—who continued bantering with each other—Tatum privately scolded Nate for leaving the bridge deck and for getting into conversations with strangers.

"That wasn't dangerous, Tatum. It was educational. You would never believe what that minister was saying."

"I do not wish to know. I just want to keep you safe from the devil we do know and the devils we don't."

All I want to do is catch them.

31

Since they had nowhere to go but back to Houdini's cabin and nothing to do there but play cards, it wasn't difficult to convince Tatum to go visiting. Nate was surprised to find the stateroom being shared by his mother, Aunt Alice, and Mrs. Houdini empty.

"Let's look for them; it's a beautiful day," he said.

"On a ship this size? With so many activities? We should get a bellboy to look for them," Tatum suggested. A bellboy would wander the ship calling out the names until the people answered and followed him back to the message sender.

"Then we'd have to sit and wait," Nate said. "Besides,

you should be seen around—considering that you are so close to making an arrest."

It didn't take very long to find them. Mrs. Houdini was singing in the lounge, accompanied on piano by one of the ship's musicians.

In a thin but sweet soprano voice, she finished the last verse of a popular song she knew by heart:

Each day I'd give the poor a thousand dollars
A diamond ring to every little queen—
O you bet your life that I would go the limit
If I were just as rich as Hetty Green.

"*Brava*, Wilhelmina the Incomparable, *brava*!" shouted Houdini, who sat in the audience.

"I was not expecting you here," Tatum said. "And my compliments to you, madam. Beautiful voice."

"The wretched storm ends, the steamer is no longer tossed like a toy, and I cannot stay away from my beautiful bride," Houdini said as he escorted Bess to a seat on a sofa next to Nate's mother. He was walking with a slight limp but not using the cane that leaned against a nearby chair.

"How I deprived the world when I asked Bess to abandon her singing career."

"You have a delightful voice, Bess," said Nate's mother. And Aunt Alice seconded that appraisal.

"Is it wise for you to be out? Alone?" the protective Tatum asked.

"Nobody cares a fig for Houdini. A day or two out of the public eye and I am forgotten."

"You would be more happy to be shot at than to be forgotten?" Mrs. Houdini asked.

"I merely mean to say that I am not in danger. That deplorable condition applies to Colonel Roosevelt, and—pardon my bluntness, ladies—to Master Fuller."

"As may be. Or may not be," Tatum said, agreeing with both sides of the proposition.

They went on at great length before finally deciding that Nate and his mother could safely enjoy some on-deck activities—chaperoned by the armed Tatum. That left the Houdinis alone with Aunt Alice, a situation pleasing to all concerned.

Nate and his mother played several games of deck shuffleboard. They watched men and women hitting golf balls into nets, but Deborah Fuller declined to watch a boxing match in the gymnasium.

"Down in third class I wager they are having a hot time today, with tug-of-war and three-legged races. I love the pillow fights myself," Tatum said.

"Why?" Nate asked.

"It's quite a sight. Two women climb onto opposite ends of a balance beam. They wrap their legs around the beam and then hit each other with pillows until one woman is knocked off."

"I suppose it is quite a sight for a man, watching women attack each other with pillows," Nate's mother said.

"Probably," Tatum agreed with embarrassment.

"Please tell Nate and me all about the fancy-dress party," she said, quickly changing the subject.

"Never been across before?"

"No, it's the first time for both of us," Nate's mother admitted. "And Aunt Alice won't hear a word said on the subject. She called it 'undignified nautical nonsense' and sent our steward away when he tried to help us prepare."

"Well, it's not like the masquerade balls that you see in London. There are lots who won't be bothered dressing up because they cannot have the dressmakers and tailors make a fancy costume. They will wear evening dress and be fashionably aloof."

"So you make your own costume?" Nate asked.

"That is the idea, making your own costume. You will not, of course," Tatum said.

"Why can't I be in disguise?" Nate protested. "Jumpy is always in disguise—we think."

"The idea is to scavenge a costume. If you want to be the Sheik of Araby, you scour likely places for rags you can use to make a turban and whatever else you need. Or you find an old mop and make a wig. Bits of rope, broken china—people find interesting bits and make up a costume. There are always some who go belowdecks and buy coal dust. To look like minstrels."

"I could find interesting things," Nate insisted.

"I do not need to remind you—"

"No, you do not need to remind my son. There will be another party on our return trip."

"But Houdini won't be aboard then."

"I am sure Houdini will not be competing for the prize," said Tatum. "He will be performing for Colonel Roosevelt. A considerably foolish endeavor with this Jumpy still on the loose."

"I can't imagine what kind of unique, one-of-a-kind illusion Houdini will perform. Since the moment he accepted the challenge, he's either been in the hospital or in bed seasick," Nate said. "Maybe he's working on it now, since he's better?"

"Actually, Nate," his mother said, "Houdini told us that he was putting the finishing touches on his demonstration while Mrs. Houdini sang earlier. What was he doing?"

"Nothing. Nothing at all that I could see."

32

Do not furrow your brow and stare. It is most disturbing," insisted Houdini.

"I'm only thinking," Nate said apologetically.

"But when your brow is furrowed and your eyes narrow, I cannot tell *what* you're thinking. That is what is disturbing."

"I was thinking that I'll hate missing the trick you have planned for tonight."

"That is not all, is it?"

Reluctantly—very reluctantly—Nate admitted it wasn't. "I want to be there when Jumpy takes the bait."

"And there are dozens of reasons you should *not* be

there: your mother's objections, the colonel's objections, Tatum's, Mrs. Houdini's. *Mine*."

"That's only five, not dozens," Nate said.

"Splitting hairs will not change our minds. You will remain here, in this stateroom, with Newborn and Charlie for company. The risk is Colonel Roosevelt's to take, not yours," Houdini said with discussion-ending finality.

Nate had realized the day before—when he read Houdini's article in the ship's newspaper—what Houdini and Roosevelt's real plan was: make Jumpy think his best opportunity to strike would be at the fancy-dress party. Thinking he was safe in disguise, Jumpy would actually walk into a foolproof trap.

But Houdini had told Nate only now—an hour before the party—that the boy could not take part in the endgame. Left out—after all Nate had done already.

He'd spent hours with an artist who sketched Jumpy in various combinations. Jumpy without makeup, Jumpy with a beard and false nose, Jumpy with a mustache and sideburns, and on and on.

Then Nate had demonstrated the gunman's walk and agitated mannerisms for the posse Tatum had recruited. This mixed group of officers and stewards—some in uniform, some in costume—would mingle with the audience during Houdini's performance. All would carry what Phin called coshes—short pipes or wooden clubs. Tatum, stationed nearest to Roosevelt, would be the last defense and the only man with a gun.

"I cannot approve civilians carrying firearms in a crowd of innocent people. This ship is under English law. It is not Dodge City or Deadwood," the inspector had said.

Now it was time for the game to begin. Houdini, with a number of chalkboard slates under his arm, was ready to leave.

Tatum made a suggestion first. "Perhaps I should carry those slates for you. Remember, you need the cane."

At the door, Houdini looked back at the forlorn trio— Nate, Phin, and Charlie—and said: "If all goes well, Nate, I will recount the event in glorious detail. I can do no better. And wedge the door, just in case."

"Rum luck, eh?" Phin said.

"Hmm . . ." was Nate's only response. They sat in silence, listening to Charlie's heavy breathing for several minutes.

"Phin, the fact is—we are the only ones who've seen what Jumpy looks like. We could spot him more easily than any of Tatum's recruits."

"As may be," Phin said, imitating the gray-haired inspector.

"So we should be there. We *must* be there!"

" 'Ow?"

"In disguise, obviously. We need disguises," Nate said.

"I don't need any. Nobody looks at bellboys. We're all the same to passengers. In-visi-ble."

173

"That's it! If I go in a bellboy suit and cap, I'll be invisible, too. Can you get me a suit? Quickly?"

"Yer glocky."

"Will you get me a suit like yours or not?"

It required more argument, and finally pleading, before Phin agreed to help. And it took nearly an hour for Phin to return to the Houdini stateroom with a bellboy suit that fitted Nate.

"Out a twig, you're ream flash," Phin said as he looked at Nate in a uniform identical to his own.

"You mean I look the part? Good, there's no time to lose."

"Not me. I'll be cashiered if anyone tumbles to you," Phin protested.

"No, you won't. I borrowed the uniform. You couldn't stop me, so you came along . . . to protect me. That's the story."

Phin protested but gave in quickly enough to the promise of the excitement ahead. They both rubbed Charlie's head and apologized before leaving the stricken-looking terrier on his own.

33

Nate thought that he could be recognized immediately by his mother, Aunt Alice, or even Mrs. Houdini. Luckily, they had been persuaded to pass the evening quietly in the otherwise empty library.

Certainly none of the other passengers gave him a second thought. One stopped him and told him to page a Mrs. Abernathy. Nate couldn't tell the passenger that he had no time to actually be a bellboy. He decided it probably didn't matter anyway. The scene on deck reminded him of a New Year's Eve celebration—all chaotic merry-making.

Some partygoers were in evening dress, but most were dressed for Halloween. Such as the man with a shirt made of signal flags sewn together. He pretended to be a jockey by riding a cane. Several women had pointed hats and broomsticks to imitate witches. A few wore borrowed nurses' uniforms. And Nate saw, as Tatum had predicted, that pretending to be a Negro was very popular. Passengers in blackface makeup were posing as everything from laundry women to shoeshine boys and railroad conductors. To Nate, there seemed something off about well-to-do tourists cavorting as servants and laborers.

Entering the lounge through different doors, Nate and Phin split up. The room was packed even though all the furniture that wasn't bolted to the floor had been removed. Roosevelt and Houdini were not there yet, providing the perfect opportunity for Nate to search. He circulated—snatching glances at faces while avoiding eye contact at all costs.

By the time he and Phin crossed paths again, Nate was positive that Jumpy was not in the room. Reverend Ludd was not in the room either, but the Lynches were—up front in seats an arm's length away from where Houdini would stand.

" 'E's likely just a barmy choker, no real 'arm in 'im," Phin said when he heard about Ludd. "Which is these Lynches?"

Nate pointed them out. Rosemary was dressed in a billowy peasant skirt. A handkerchief was wrapped around her head. Jackie was in a pirate's costume—complete with black eye patch and sheathed sword hanging from his waist.

"Where do you think he got that sword?" Nate asked.

"There's some onboard, ceremonial like, but 'e must 'ave brought 'is own. No dicky'd lend 'im 'is."

"Why would a street cleaner own a sword?"

"You said 'e's gonna be lord of the manor in Ireland. Maybe 'e's takin' up fencin'."

Applause told them Roosevelt and Houdini were entering. Nate and Phin both turned away, trying to make themselves invisible.

"Good even-ning, Layyy-deees and Gen-tell-mennn!" Houdini said in a voice loud enough to stop stampeding animals. As the performer explained the purpose of the evening's entertainment, Nate again surveyed the room's layout.

The spacious first-class lounge was a rectangular room with four exit doors. Two forward doors led to the grand stairway—the route Jumpy had used after his first attack. Two rear doors opened onto alleyways that led to the smoking room. Crewmen carrying concealed clubs lingered—one near each door—trying to appear casual. Nate knew that there were several additional armed men in the room, but they seemed swallowed up by the crowd.

Houdini leaned on his cane near the forward wall and stood next to a circular table. Roosevelt stood nearby, Tatum behind him.

Nate, facing forward, was behind and to the side of a tall man. He was close enough to be seen by Houdini or Tatum if the man moved. Being there would not be a problem, Nate told himself, if Jumpy was captured. But if nothing happened, having defied all the adults he knew onboard the ship would definitely cause him trouble.

Seeking a path to safety, Nate dropped to his knees and worked his way to the back of the Lynches' sofa. The passengers he jostled were amused by the sight of a bellboy trying to get the best possible view. Crouched against the sofa—behind Jackie Lynch's head—Nate could both see the demonstration and turn to get a view of the room behind him.

"This evening's mystification will utilize slate boards, the kind you used as a child in grammar school," Houdini declared. "I am sure that many of you have witnessed so-called spirit writing during séances, but this will be *completely* different. The lights will remain on. The chalkboards will never be out of your sight. I will have *no* opportunity to use sleight of hand to influence the results."

"We'll be watching you like hawks!" shouted an onlooker.

"I sincerely hope that you do," Houdini said. He took sheets of paper, envelopes, and pencils from the table next to him. "Steward, please distribute these," he said. "Give a pencil, a slip of paper, and an envelope to each of five people you choose randomly in the crowd. Colonel Roosevelt, I will give you the same writing equipment. Please, write nothing yet."

The steward moved through the crowd with great difficulty. Everyone in the lounge wanted to participate. And it was then, above the murmur of the audience, that Nate heard something disturbing.

"Bill! You can't, Bill," Rosemary Lynch whispered harshly to her husband—who was supposedly named Jackie.

Jackie-Bill Lynch hissed something back in response.

"Bill, we've worked too hard to throw it all away," she whispered angrily. "*He* is not our only enemy."

Nate's suspicions about the couple came rushing back. He was certain now that his original hunch was correct! But how to warn Houdini and the colonel?

"I want each of you, including the colonel, to write down a question about President Roosevelt you would like answered," Houdini said. "Before you write, I beg, do not make the question one that can be easily answered. For example, do not ask how old the colonel is or where he lives or his horse's name. The question should be one that only the colonel himself can answer. Are we agreed? Good. When you have written your question, seal it in the envelope and make a mark on the envelope you will be able to recognize."

President Roosevelt cupped his slip in the palm of his

hand to keep it away from Houdini's line of sight. Houdini leaned over, picked up a book lying on the table, and handed it to Roosevelt.

"This will make it easier to write and prevent me from seeing the movement of your hand, Colonel."

Seeing this gave Nate an idea. He patted his coat and felt notepaper and pencils inside.

Lucky a bellboy must carry pencils and paper.

Nate stared at the blank paper before composing the clearest message he could:

Pirate (Mr. Lynch) IS Jumpy's boss. Fear he may use sword to kill Roosevelt if Jumpy doesn't. Peasant woman (Mrs. Lynch) in on it. Nate Fuller

But how to get it to them?

The steward returned with five sealed envelopes and placed them in a hat Houdini had borrowed from an audience member. As Roosevelt deposited his sealed envelope in the hat, Houdini returned the book to the table. He stood there silently, with his back to the room, as anticipation grew.

Nate cast his eyes around, hoping to see Phin. Instead he saw a man in torn coveralls, carrying a shovel and a pail. His face, smeared with soot, made the man look just like one of the ship's coal stokers, except for one thing— the purple wart on his nose. Jumpy's wart was only partially covered with soot.

Houdini turned toward the crowd and said: "Colonel, can you verify that I did not observe you writing your question? And then verify that I have not touched the envelope in which you placed it?"

Roosevelt answered yes to both questions.

"Sir, will you retrieve your question from the hat and bring it here?"

Nate decided his best—his only—chance was then. As Roosevelt fished his hand in the hat, having some difficulty finding his sheet of paper, Nate played the "invisibility of servants" card. He rose and walked stiffly around the couch and straight up to a startled Tatum. Hand out, palm up, he offered Tatum the note he had written, bowed slightly, and backed away. Edging along the wall toward Jumpy, Nate was certain neither the Lynches nor Jumpy had seen his face. When he looked forward, he saw Tatum staring at the message.

"Now I will pick the two slates up from this table," Houdini said. "I demonstrate that both slates are completely blank."

Houdini held up the slates, first to the left side of the audience, then to the right. All four sides of the slates were blank. Holding them together, parallel to the floor, Houdini asked Roosevelt, "Sir, be kind enough to slide the envelope with your question, and a piece of chalk, between the two slates. Ensure that I do not touch the envelope."

Roosevelt complied, obviously absorbed in the unfolding illusion. The normally talkative former president was as silent as the rest of the audience.

"Finally, I hold these slates together with only my fingers. Colonel, be so kind as to seal them with the rubber bands before you."

After that was done, Houdini delicately placed the slates on the table.

Nate had jostled his way through the crowd, to the great annoyance of several passengers. He moved directly alongside the soot-smeared assassin without Jumpy noticing. Jumpy was just watching the display like the rest of the audience. Nate and Tatum were probably the only persons there not absorbed in the show.

"Allow me to concentrate a few moments. I will wave my hands *above* the slates. Everyone, please observe that I *never* touch the slates," Houdini said.

After less than a minute, Houdini backed away from the table and looked about the room triumphantly. "Colonel, kindly tell everyone the exact words you wrote on a slip of paper, sealed in an envelope, and yourself placed between the slates."

"I asked where I was last Christmas," Roosevelt said.

"And you think that is a difficult question to answer?"

"Because I was on an expedition to Brazil that only my family knew about," the former president replied. "All of my companions on that trip are in South America. And, as it happens, on Christmas Day we were in a previously unmapped and unnamed part of the country deep in the Amazonian jungle."

"That would be exceptionally difficult for me to guess, I suppose," Houdini said, coyly looking around the room.

"Absolutely *impossible*, I'd say."

"May I ask the name of the precise location you camped on Christmas Day?" Houdini continued.

"Indeed! My party spent the day along the River of Doubt. Not a location you could take a wild guess at and hit."

"Indeed, not a location one could easily guess." Houdini sighed, bowing his head.

"No one could know. The trip was a closely held secret," Roosevelt said. "It's a dreadful shame that your demonstration has failed, but—"

"But, Colonel, you have not yet opened the slates."

Roosevelt did, removing the rubber bands and lifting up the top slate.

"I'll be . . . I don't know what I will be!" Roosevelt exclaimed. "You are better than your reputation, Houdini. I am positively stunned!"

When Houdini asked the former president to hold the slate up for the audience, Tatum slipped past him and handed Nate's note to Houdini. As the audience applauded frantically and shouted their appreciation, Nate could see that his eyes were cast downward.

Even from his distant location, Nate could clearly see an outline of Brazil drawn in chalk. A large white dot denoted a place in the Amazon jungle area. And next to the dot was written "The River of Doubt."

"In the name of Heaven, Houdini, how *did* you do it?" Roosevelt demanded. "Do you really have psychic powers? Is it telepathy?"

Houdini smiled. The smile broadened into a wide grin. Then he snapped his fingers in the air.

"It's all . . . just . . . hocus-pocus."

34

As Nate watched, Jumpy took several deep breaths and straightened himself. *He must know that it's now or never.* He dropped the coal shovel by his side and reached into the pail—Nate guessed—to retrieve his revolver. The room was seething with excitement. Nobody but Nate even noticed that he did indeed extract a gun.

Jumpy pushed his way forward. Remembering the colonel's advice—"Do not hit a man unless you can put him to sleep"—Nate picked up the abandoned shovel and followed. When he had enough room for a clean swing, Nate arched the coal shovel above his head and brought it down as heavily as he could—flat on Jumpy's shoulder. The gunman crumpled to the floor.

Nate cried out for help and grabbed Jumpy's gun. The two guards stationed at the far end of the lounge were there in seconds and took possession of the fallen gunman and his weapon.

Pandemonium enveloped the room as passengers realized what had happened. Most were too panicked to understand that the danger was over. They practically clawed one another to flee the room, leaving a path open to where Houdini, Roosevelt, and Tatum stood.

Nate saw that the Lynches were almost the only passengers not fleeing. Mrs. Lynch seemed to be tugging at her husband, trying to pull him away. Mr. Lynch stood casually, his weight on one hip, his hand on the sword's hilt.

As Nate told himself that Lynch couldn't be crazy enough to try anything, the pirate whipped his sword from its scabbard, raised it overhead, and plunged it downward at Roosevelt's neck. Before the former president or Tatum could respond, the blow was blocked by Houdini's cane. Holding it parallel to the ground, one hand at each end, Houdini had jumped forward and thrust the cane between the sword and its target.

"Drop that sword! I will shoot!" Tatum said loudly, his gun drawn.

Lynch ignored the warning and actually pulled the sword free from Houdini's cane. The madman stumbled back, but then lunged forward as he recovered his balance.

Tatum fired. The shock blew Lynch backward, and he

fell, still clutching his sword. Mrs. Lynch dropped to the floor beside her husband. "You've killed him!" she cried.

It's all over, thought Nate.

He was wrong. A commotion erupted behind him. The costumed stewards holding on to Jumpy were so distracted by Lynch's attack that he correctly sensed a chance to escape. And he had an escape route planned.

Jerking free from his captors, Jumpy dashed straight for one of the knee-high to ceiling stained-glass windows that ringed the room. Turning and jumping at the last instant, he smashed through the window and rolled onto the promenade deck outside.

"After 'im!" Phin cried, and dashed for the window.

Nate followed, unwilling to hear Houdini frantically shouting, "Stop, Nate! Stop!"

Nate glimpsed Phin running to the stern at breakneck speed and followed. He could hear a couple of the posse members following farther behind.

Moments later Nate saw Jumpy stop near the rear railing of the first-class promenade. The assassin had to give up or jump the gap that separated first class from second class. Phin was on him so fast that he couldn't have expected the sucker punch Jumpy threw.

As Phin reeled, holding his gut, Jumpy took a running start. He leaped onto the railing, bounded across, and landed clumsily on the adjoining deck.

Nate arrived, trying to pull Phin to his feet.

"Don't stop," Phin sputtered. "Chase that brassy sod."

Nate considered the jump and said, "In for a penny . . ." Then he took a running start, vaulted the rail, and leaped—churning his legs as Jumpy had done before him. Rolling on the deck, he finished his thought: ". . . in for a pound." As he looked into the distance, Nate could trace Jumpy's path through the shaking fists and yells of angry partygoers. Then he glimpsed the assassin hanging over the deck's rail and letting go—dropping to the deck below. Nate followed close behind.

Standing up, he saw Jumpy dropping yet another deck. Nate followed again. This time he landed badly, twisting his ankle.

"I can't lose him now, not now," Nate said to himself as he tried hopping forward. But a few painful steps told him that his pursuit was over. Catching his breath, he heard Phin cry, "Ahoy below!" He turned and saw his friend land behind him.

"I lost him," Nate said.

"Lord love a duck! Look, ya' treed him like a dog chasin' a cat," Phin said, pointing skyward.

It was true. Jumpy was standing atop a railing at the extreme rear end of the ship, clinging to a flagpole. Below him were the wake of the ship and the blackness of the ocean at night.

"It ain't a 'angin' offense! Ten years on the moors is all . . . then you'll be a bleedin' 'ero to every barm fly ya know!" Phin shouted to Jumpy. The voices of the posse could be heard in the distance.

"I can't go to prison," Jumpy replied, more to himself than to Nate or Phin.

"Prison can't be as bad as dying," Nate insisted. "You'll get a fresh start. You're not a killer."

"Listen to the lad," Tatum said, gun in hand and leading the pursuit. "Come down or we will go up for you."

"I can't go to prison," Jumpy repeated sadly. He leaned back, let loose his grip, and fell, swallowed up first by darkness, then by the sea.

35

Houdini threatened to box Nate's ears for disobeying everybody. Instead, he whisked him back to his stateroom so the limping youth could change and return to his own cabin.

"If your mother and your great-aunt catch wind of what happened tonight, you will be packed off to a military school to learn discipline, they will never speak to my wife again, and I will never live that down. There are no options. I *must* make certain you get no credit for what you did tonight. Does that seem fair to you?"

"It doesn't, but if you think it's the only way, it must be," Nate said, trying to shake off his disappointment.

"What an excellent young man you are! Now go like

the wind. And keep your mother and Aunt Alice away from people. I must see the colonel, the captain, Tatum, the newspaper editor . . . and I think I will go visit brave Flanagan to help hasten his recovery with the news."

Deborah Fuller's attitude told Nate that she suspected she was not getting the whole story. But she knew it was far better to learn the truth later on and keep Aunt Alice permanently in the dark. In fact, she cheerfully agreed to let Nate spend the next morning—their last before docking—with Houdini.

"Try not to get into any *more* trouble," she advised while Aunt Alice was in the washroom.

He ran into Mrs. Houdini outside the door.

"*Ach*, you men! My husband has sent me to keep your mother and Aunt Alice out of trouble until we dock."

"Thank you so much," Nate said. "But I think my mother has some idea."

"Of course she would. You are so smart that you do not yet appreciate her. Someday! As my husband likes to say. Go now, he is packing. But wait, I have a note for you from President Roosevelt. Very hush-hush. He couldn't let a bellboy give it to the wrong person by mistake."

Nate ripped open the envelope and read eagerly as he walked:

Dear Nate,
To say that I owe you my eternal gratitude is an entirely inadequate expression. And I heartily applaud

your modification of my favorite West African proverb: I will always be in your debt for speaking softly and carrying a big shovel. Remember the last part of the proverb: The man who speaks softly and carries a big shovel will go *exceedingly* far in life.

Your father was an honorable, idealistic man—and you are obviously his son. You are brave but not foolish. You have grit, resolution, and a nimble mind. One day all the world will know it.

Yours faithfully,

Theodore Roosevelt

P.S. Since your family will not be available to meet mine this Christmas in Oyster Bay, I offer you (and the Houdinis!) an open invitation. Perhaps next July 4 or the Christmas following that. I do fondly wish that we gather again in happier circumstances.

"A noble spirit, a generous one, too!" Houdini commented after Nate showed him Roosevelt's note. "What bully fun that party will be."

"I doubt that Tatum or Phin will be there," Nate said regretfully.

"Ocean voyages often make for brief but intense friendships—but rarely as intense as ours have been this time across the pond."

"I wonder if I will ever see them again," Nate said.

"You'll likely see Tatum on your return trip. He's thoroughly ready to put down his pistol and pick up his playing cards again. And if Phin spends some of my lavish tip on the elocution books I have recommended, he may be a steward by then."

They laughed together, and Nate said, "I had better say goodbye to both of them before we dock. I might not recognize them otherwise, on the return trip."

They worked silently awhile, repacking all the books Houdini had unpacked but never had time to read. Finally, Nate decided to pump his friend for information—starting with the Lynches.

"They clearly are not who they pretended to be. Even though he's dead, she refuses to talk. But I am sure Captain Root will sort the story out eventually."

"Where do you think the real Lynches are?" Nate asked.

"They came to a bad end, I fear. Only because they made the acquaintance of the criminals who impersonated them is my guess," Houdini said, shaking his head.

Nate asked another question that he thought Houdini would answer.

"Mrs. Houdini seemed very unhappy about doing your mind-reading trick the other day. Why is that?"

"Hmmm, I will tell you. That kind of act produces a bad effect. Sometimes, a very bad effect," Houdini said.

"It astonished everybody who saw it."

"That is true, but you see, we know enough not to hurt people with our phony telepathy. Years ago, when we could barely scratch out a living, we did mind reading to get bookings. Unpleasant things happened, people were hurt—quite unintentionally."

"How?" Nate asked.

"Another time, not now."

Nate said nothing more. He was reluctant to ask the really big question.

"Of course, you want to know how I did the slate trick, yes?"

"I certainly do," Nate said.

"But you know that you are not supposed to ask *that* question," Houdini said.

"I know, but it was so incredible. Did the colonel figure it out?"

"He never will or could," replied Houdini. "It was too simple for a great mind to understand."

"I don't have a great mind, but I don't think I will ever figure it out, either."

"Sit a moment, Nate," Houdini said with a wave of his hand. "I believe that disloyalty in trusted servants is the most disheartening thing that can happen to a public performer. My secret methods have been steadily shielded by the strict integrity of my assistants. Can you imagine why?"

"You trust only trustworthy people, I guess."

"Such is life. And I make them swear a lifetime oath of secrecy. An oath never, for any reason, to reveal the secrets they have learned. When we married, Bess swore that oath to me."

"You're joking, aren't you? You made Mrs. Houdini swear an oath of secrecy?"

"I most certainly did," Houdini said. "Nate, if you wish to be part of Houdini's inner circle, Houdini's family, look into my eyes."

He stared fixedly at Nate, his blue-gray eyes practically boring holes through Nate's.

"Now say 'I do solemnly swear on my sacred honor as a man that as long as I live I shall never divulge the secrets of Harry Houdini. So help me God almighty and may he keep me steadfast.' "

"Yes . . . of course I swear."

"You *solemnly* swear?"

"I do."

Houdini's attitude lightened as he said, "Good. I will tell you then. First, nobody knew in advance that the colonel was making this trip."

"That's right," Nate agreed.

"Nobody knew but Houdini."

"How did you find out?"

"Days before we sailed, I contacted a friend of mine—the purser of this ship—to ask if anything 'interesting' was likely on the voyage. He told me the colonel had secretly booked a stateroom and bound me to secrecy. I was happy to oblige. At the same time, I knew that the colonel had written a series of articles scheduled to appear in next month's *New York Herald*."

Nate gave his complete attention to the story while having no idea what Houdini's point would be.

"I rushed to the newspaper's office and convinced a reporter-friend to let me peek at the articles privately—very hush-hush. I read that Colonel Roosevelt had been on a surveying expedition to Brazil last winter. Roosevelt wrote that, on Christmas Day, he had camped on the River of Doubt. That was all I needed."

"So you drew the map on the slate before we ever left New York," Nate deduced.

"Excellent."

"And you only pretended to show us that all four sides were blank?"

"Nothing more than run-of-the-mill sleight of hand. One hundred percent effective nonetheless," Houdini replied.

"But how did the rest of it work?" Nate asked.

"I coaxed the colonel into asking me to perform an illusion moments after I met him—moments before Jumpy introduced himself to us. But from that point on, it was mere child's play."

"But you never touched the colonel's question. How could you tell that he asked the right question?"

"Hocus-pocus, all hocus-pocus. Remember, I worked very hard to plant the suggestion that everyone should ask a personal, unusual question. I knew from reading the articles that the president's Christmas Day spent on the River of Doubt loomed large in his thoughts. I merely forced the thought front and center. As a backup, I had six envelopes in my pocket, all asking 'Where did I spend last Christmas?' If the colonel asked the wrong question, I would have switched my questions for the real questions."

"But you didn't have to make a switch because you knew he asked the right question, yes?"

"You remember when we were in the lounge yesterday? My darling wife was singing. There were two books on a table near the front of the room—the table I used last night. I borrowed those books after you and your mother left the lounge, excused myself from my wife and your great-aunt, and took the books to my suite. Using a razor, I slit open the covers. Into each cover I inserted a piece of carbon paper and a piece of typing paper. You remember that I passed the colonel one of those books last night, suggesting that it would be easier to write that way? As he then folded his question and sealed it in the envelope, I retrieved the book, slid the typing paper out while my back was to the audience, and saw that he had done precisely what I had hoped for."

"Wow! That's more than hocus-pocus. That is genius," Nate said admiringly. "Either way you couldn't fail."

"Preparation and practice can make geniuses of us all."

The *Lusitania*'s horns bellowed suddenly. A steward walked by outside, hitting his gong and announcing that the ship would be arriving in Liverpool soon. Nate realized that he had completely forgotten about the European adventure he had so eagerly anticipated only five days before. He scarcely believed that he had been on the ship only five days.

"These five days have been like five months to me," Houdini said, seemingly reading Nate's thoughts again. "Make the most of this trip, Nate. Savor every second. You should have goals—a mission—to accomplish on each great journey you take."

"Do you have a mission, I mean, a mission beyond entertaining a million people?"

"I do indeed," Houdini said with a smile. "My mother asked specially for a gift: 'Warm woolen slippers, size six.' "

"That's all she wants?"

"The desire for things wanes as you age. I feel it already. Mind you, I'm not done yet! But when I'm too old to perform, I'll retire and spend all my time writing about the history of magic."

"You will *never* be too old to fight crime and help people—not with me around."

"We can never really tell what will happen, can we?"

AUTHOR'S NOTE

In 1911, when this story takes place, having the biggest and fastest ocean liner was a source of national pride. Governments funded shipbuilding and ship maintenance, even though the ships were privately owned by profit-making companies. But those subsidies had strings attached. When World War I broke out, in 1914, the British-owned Cunard Line agreed that the *Lusitania* and her sister ship, the *Mauretania*, would carry troops and munitions for His Majesty in time of war.

That decision made the *Lusitania* a target of German U-boat submarines. She was torpedoed off the Irish coast in 1915 and sank in less than twenty minutes. Over one thousand passengers and crew members were killed.

But when she was launched, in 1906, the *Lusitania* was the longest (787 feet), fastest (twenty-six knots per hour), and most technologically advanced ship ever built. And the most expensive to travel on. In 1911, American police officers and university professors made about $1,500 yearly. A five-day trip in one of the *Lusitania*'s best suites cost $4,000.

I located my story on the *Lusitania* because so much written and visual material—including deck-by-deck floor plans—is available to help make the trip vivid and historically accurate. (A 1907 book titled *Lusitania: The Cunard Turbine-Driven Quadruple-Screw Atlantic Liner* has all the technical information conceivable and more than fifty interior and exterior photographs. Many public libraries have copies of that book.)

In this second adventure about Nate and Houdini, I attempt, within reason, to fairly and faithfully represent real people. Much of what is said by both Roosevelt and Houdini is quoted or paraphrased from their actual words. Some deviations from historical fact have been taken to advance the story.

Houdini and former president Theodore Roosevelt did meet (in 1914) on an Atlantic crossing, but it was not the *Lusitania*. Roosevelt discussed mental telepathy with Houdini. Houdini performed the "River of Doubt" slate trick exactly as described— much to Roosevelt's astonishment and pleasure. Houdini later visited the Roosevelt home in Oyster Bay, New York, and performed for the former president's grandchildren.

Nobody shot at Roosevelt during that trip, but an assassination attempt was made in 1912. Shot at close range, the former president survived because the bullet was slowed down by a thick sheaf of papers inside his coat.

All steamship lines employed undercover operatives such as the retired inspector Arthur Tatum. That was necessary because the normal etiquette of society was suspended during transatlantic voyages. Aboard ship, people did—and still do—establish friendships quickly and easily. Well-mannered confidence men and cardsharps took small fortunes from their marks until undercover detectives unmasked and arrested them.

Captain Railsback is an entirely fictional character—an archetype of imperious ships' captains through the ages. Railsback should not be compared with the real captain of the *Lusitania*, William Thomas Turner.

In the early 1800s, English textile workers who claimed to be followers of an imaginary "King Ludd" vandalized factories in a desperate attempt to preserve their jobs. My Reverend Jeremiah Ludd is also imaginary. He represents that group of people— threatened by new ideas and scientific discoveries—who vainly try to turn back the clock of history. Ludd's words are taken from actual period writings and sermons. There really were people who wanted to blow up ships like the *Lusitania* and fill the subway tunnels for religious reasons. (Incidentally, English literature since the 1400s has referred to Gotham—Ludd's home—as a village notable for its abundance of fools.)

The anarchist assassins—Jumpy and the couple impersonating the Lynches—likewise are fictional. Their fanatical beliefs and willingness to use murder as a weapon of terror were as real then as they are today, unfortunately.

The song Bess sings about Hetty Green was very popular. Hetty Green was a successful Wall Street investor at a time when no other women were active in the finanical world. A frequent subject of both news and gossip, Ms. Green was disparagingly called the Witch of Wall Street.

Lastly, a few words about the illusions in the book.

The magicians' unwritten code demands that the mechanics of illusions never be revealed to outsiders. Houdini made his own rules about most things, that rule included.

Houdini never revealed—or had any desire to reveal—the secrets of illusionists he respected, such as Harry Kellar and Chung Ling Soo. They were honest practitioners of entertaining deceit. But Houdini was relentless in exposing the dozens of performers who traded on his name (calling themselves Kleppini, Whodini, Undini, et cetera) and used rigged props to perform pale imitations of Houdini's illusions.

Meticulous preparation and attention to detail were the hallmarks of Houdini's craft. He rightly felt that he put too much time and effort into his work to have it counterfeited. And if he wished to expose *his own* methods — as he did a number of times — that was his prerogative.

I had Houdini explain the "River of Doubt" slate trick to Nate because he himself publicly revealed how it was done at a later date.

After her husband's death, Bess Houdini inadvertently divulged the secret of the mind-reading or second-sight act. It was done through a simple numerical code tied to long, memorized lists of objects. The coded words were conveyed by formulaic phrases.

To tell Houdini the date on former president Roosevelt's coin, Bess says "I pray you concentrate before you *try to* tell me the date this coin was minted, please, I urge you to take your time."

Houdini correctly guesses 1678 because *pray* equaled 1, *concentrate* equaled 6, *please* equaled 7, and *urge* equaled 8. Because the word *try*, used alone, equaled the number five, Bess emphasizes the words *try to* to indicate that *try* is not being used as code.

They had also assigned numbers to long lists of objects that a man or woman might reasonably carry in a wallet or purse. Of course, Bess made certain to pick only objects that were on their memorized list. So guesswork was unnecessary if both partners were well-practiced and had excellent memories.

Of course, other performers doing the same act perfected their own codes. One was synchronized counting cued by sound. The partner holding the object would make a sound that started both partners counting silently but in unison. When the female partner in that act died, it took the remaining partner four years to find another assistant who could silently count in unison with him.

Finally, Houdini used several names for the needle-swallowing trick, but never revealed how he did it. And I will not second-guess his judgment.

The oath of secrecy Nate swears is the oath Houdini required of all who joined his inner circle. Houdini's brothers took the oath, as did Bess when she joined his act. All Houdini's stage assistants, carpenters, and metal workers were required to swear the oath. While many of them eventually quit the act and moved on to other jobs, none ever broke the oath.